Hand of Belenos

Mickey Stone

Stone Literary LLC

This is a work of fiction woven through real places.

The River Earn flows through Crieff, Scotland. The James River winds through Virginia. The Graham and Drummond clans have deep roots in Highland history. These places and names are real, and they are honored here.

But the characters who walk these lands, the events that unfold along these rivers, and the gifts passed through these bloodlines are born of imagination. Any resemblance to actual persons, living or dead, is purely coincidental.

McKenna Chapel, Dugald Wynd, and McKenna's Glen exist in the heart of this story, if not on any map.

James Bend, it's surroundings and the James Bend Medical Center are also born of imagination. Any resemblance to actual persons, living or dead, is purely coincidental.

Book Cover by Tom Elliot, TG GRAPHICS

Illustrations by Mickey Stone

First Edition - 2025

Book ONE, from "The Venerated Legacy" series.

Acknowledgements

Nick O. – For lighting a fire within me.

Elizabeth Hahn Matis – Advisor, Beta Reader, and for being totally honest in her approach.

Tom Elliot – For nailing the cover art.

My Beta Readers: Matthew John, Jean M., Mason T.

To Alexandra, without your patience and understanding, none of this would exist.

Contents

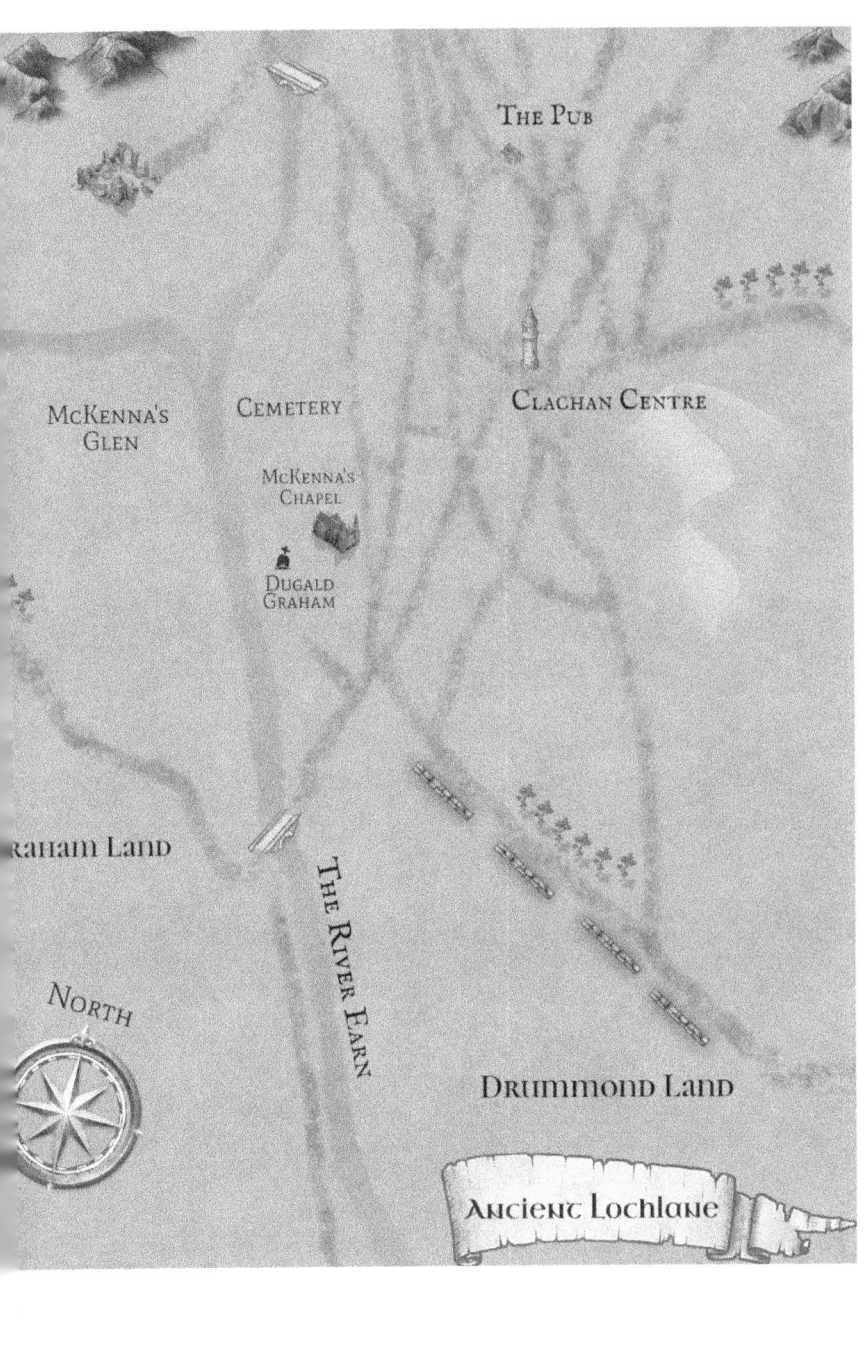

Many have crossed the river.

Few have stopped to hear its witness.

Chapter One

T HE WIND ALONG THE RIVER EARN sliced like an
unseen dagger. Whipping from North to South,
the tempest sent a chill through everyone who ventured
out that day, Clan be damned. Folks in the surrounding
villages bundled up, shielding themselves from the cold,
and it only promised to worsen.

Late fall, the leaves were stripped from the trees. They
stood like barren giants in the distance on the hills.
Nothing to stop the winds from blowing down from the
mountains.

Dugald pulled his deerskin wraps tighter and clasped
the Penannular bearing the Graham Clan Badge. It held
the skins over his shoulders and around his neck. The
gusts filled unseen voids.

*This winter will be hard. Our harvest crop, plentiful
most seasons, failed us.* Dugald searched the skies. *Many
have so little, help each other, we will.*

It's always been this way in the Highlands. Difficult
winters. Difficult weather. Difficult harvest. Difficult

decisions. "Do I feed the cattle that later feeds me?" Dugald pondered out loud. His breath fogged in the bitter air. "Or do I feed my family?"

" 'Tis an impossible decision." A new, unnerving choice hung over the valley.

Drummond hands labored these fields for centuries. Sound men. A clan built on strength. Now, the Graham Clan came down from the western mountains. He gazed to his right, towards the hills, then back to the Drummond Village in the east.

In the distance, a wisp of smoke from a chimney rose to the heavens.

"They're weak. We haven't brought our wood in yet." Dugald scoffed under his breath.

But they've worked the earth for hundreds of years. Through the skirmishes when the Graham Clan first arrived. Through the uneasy agreements between the two to exist together in this lush but harsh landscape.

"God d'int mean for us to perish, but He d'int mean for them to be so close." Unpleasant memories were like the gusts in the air, plentiful and bitter.

"We couldn't rid ourselves of the British Drummond bloke last year. What a belligerent sot he proved to be. He must've come from their village. Glad we sent him on his way—back to London. Godspeed to the likes of him!"

Dugald reached his destination, the only pub in the county—the only neutral place where men can be men and steel themselves from the misery of the early winter and block the blabbering of women and the bickering of children always underfoot.

Dugald entered and settled at a corner table near several members of the Drummond clan—*if closer their odor might pierce my nostrils.* He cast his eyes out the window beyond.

A few wore their Drummond tartan, and the flames danced, keeping the room warm. Dugald gritted his teeth and begrudgingly admitted—the chill left his weathered face.

They kept to themselves, ignoring Dugald—*fine with me.* All he wanted was to be left alone and drink his mead.

One of the rabble announced, "Why 'ave the fire? Go out like a newborn and frolic the day away!" Angus chirped, "Bollocks, Fergus! Bleating like a crippled goat, you, to be sure!"

Manly humor and banter—it didn't change, no matter your clan affiliation. Man bests man—or dares one to do better. A smirk came to Dugald's face.

At the Drummond table, a man caught Dugald's eye—*keeping to himself, like me.*

When the rancor settled down, Dugald overheard him say, "It's been two years, two years since I lost my two bairns—precious to me. And now? My oldest is sick. I fear he caught the Scarlet. My thought is he won't make the winter. T'is a sadness I canna bear, lads..." his voice trailed off.

His clanmates kept silent and respectful.

Winter in the valley? Punishing, and their bones would bear witness to its cruelty. The spartan cemetery nearby had its share of souls buried within who could speak to it.

As Dugald sat, focusing on gnarled fingers gripping the cup, he felt a tug. Not on his clothing or even his arm, but from within, not a slight feeling, but one that bore power. He looked around, but no one was present.

Do not ignore the pull when it calls to you...

He recalled words that had swirled in the dreams that haunted his nights.

Answer the pull when it bids you to follow...

He didn't understand that which was pulling him. He

saw nothing. He observed nothing. All around was the same, yet the pull grew stronger.

Answer the pull at a slight cost to you. Do not answer the pull begets a greater cost to all...

Dugald could no longer ignore what he heard, both within his head and from around him. He stood, walked to the man, who studied him up and down with a harsh eye.

His voice changed from fatherly-tinged sorrow to one of utter disdain. "Ha' ye come to gloat, Graham?" he sneered.

The remaining Drummond clansmen arose from their seats, uncovering their broadswords in their sheaths. The floor would feast upon his blood if he broached the line.

Dugald spoke with purpose, "Aye, we stand with opposite clans, but together as men." The furrow in his brow framed the seriousness of his words.

"Take me to y'er boy. We've not the time to ponder..."

The Drummond male stared in disbelief, but Dugald stood resolute. His words bore the honor that both respected.

Kieran Drummond rose and obliged the request.

T he group travelled down the path to a humble structure. Kieran said, "This be me hooze. The boy be upstairs." Coughing echoed from above them as the door opened. The Drummond men's eyes fixed on Dugald like hawks on the hunt. They prayed for a reason to lay blade to skin.

As the group stepped inside, Dugald turned to Kieran and said, "I g' my word, no harm will come t'the boy. T'will be alright." Kieran could not deny him, but could not believe him. The Drummond men started forward to stop Dugald, but Kieran raised his hand and stopped them from moving closer.

Dugald stared back at the group, wheeled, and disappeared up the stairs. Footsteps... muffled voices... then the coughing stopped.

Confusion came over the group's faces. *What transpired? Is all lost? Why is it so quiet? Pray—the wind ceased howling!*

They traded stares, then moved as one towards the stairs when the running of feet across the floorboards froze them where they stood.

Down the stairs came the son, in his bedclothes! The child ran to his mother and embraced her. "Mother!" he cried, turning. "Father!" They stood in stunned awe. Fergus clutched the crucifix hanging around his neck and kissed it.

Dugald struggled down the stairs. He stepped in front of the group. They parted, revealing Kieran holding his child, tears streaming down his face. Dugald limped to him, reached out, grasped his forearm, and said, "We be on opposite Clans, but this is a gift I can give but this once. Once through your door, opposite clans we must return."

He walked past the others. They bowed their heads—reaching out to touch his outer deerskin wrap as he passed. Angus blessed himself after touching his sleeve.

Dugald moved through the door, using the frame to steady his weak legs. Now outside, he turned back for one last survey of the awestruck Drummond men.

Kieran raised his hand towards him. His eyes had disbelief etched upon them. Dugald nodded his head, then set his sights on his village ... and disappeared down the path.

————◆○◆————

Chapter Two

T HE SUMMER SUN beat down on Duncan's face.

Working in his yard ranked high among his favorite things to do—not confined by walls, a classroom, a gym or a locker room. Alone in the open air, with no phones, no rabbit-eared televisions, nothing to take his focus from the job at hand.

But this? At 11 years old? *Mom sentenced me to yard prison, with hard labor no less.*

Mulch. Piles of it. No—mountains. Still, he loved the aroma. The pine and bark... that earthy outdoor aroma called to him. It filled his lungs as he drew a deep breath.

"Mom!!"

"Moooom!!!"

McKenna stuck her head out the kitchen window.

"Do I have to spread all of this? It'll take forever! I wanted to go play with Timmy!"

"Duncan Graham, you get to work or I'll call the lad and his family t' tell them where t' come for your waaake! Sure as y'er standin' there, I'll dig the grave myself!" Her Scottish accent snapped through the air.

Duncan understood that when that voice cracked like a whip, no back-talking or arguments happened. You do what Mom says. You do it now, not later. Duncan knew the rules. *She always made up for raising her voice like that. Maybe this time she will make cookies as a surprise.* He hoped so anyway.

"Yes, Ma'am," he answered as he positioned the wheelbarrow to put in the first load. Shovelful after shovelful, wheel the load over to her prized flower bed, spread it out on his hands and knees.

He ran the checklist in his head nonstop—ten times.

Uhhh. Oooh boooy.

Not a good day to wear a bright colored T-shirt. Duncan stared down at the soiled garment—then peeled it off. The sun warmed his skin and made it glisten in the sunlight. Sweat matted his long, wavy brown hair. The sun twinkled off the red highlights.

If I am working outside, I might as well tan.

So lucky I don't burn... He didn't have the typical pasty white Scottish complexion.

Duncan had heard the name 'Black Scot' before, but he didn't understand it at first. Having a darker complexion and dark tresses ranked high on the list of lucky traits. Duncan never sunburned. Ever.

Five hours on the beach, and everyone else would dash for cover or sunscreen. Duncan was immovable, throwing his frisbee around with the dog in the sweltering heat.

His mother wrapped her pride in her "Little Dark Warrior" like a shawl on her shoulders. Blessed from birth, something that defied odds, yet here he stood. A gift. A blessing. A...

"Haaaay!" Duncan glanced up to see Timmy.
"Heeeey!" Duncan leapt up and started play-fighting with his friend.

Timmy backed up and raised his fists. Prepared and ready, complete with his meanest face, he dropped his crutch to the side and waited to get tackled.

Down they went, laughing, rolling and wrestling. Duncan took care, knowing Timmy's legs lacked strength...but somehow, Timmy always won. They both knew Duncan let him win, but they didn't care.

This was livin'. This was summer. This is the way life is supposed to be.

He remembered back to when Timmy was stronger. Playing catch, his arm ranked as one of the best on the block. And Duncan constantly challenged him to try and throw farther, adding a little distance each time. Timmy never failed.

One time, though, Timmy couldn't. The ball fell well short of where he stood. So Duncan baited him to do it again. It came up short again. And again. And again.

Timmy must have been tired or something. Duncan mentioned it in passing. Timmy admitted to being sore for a week or so. They didn't think anything of it.

A couple of weeks later, out on the tire swing, the two of them goofing around—Timmy fell off—crashed really hard on his back. It scared him more than it hurt. Duncan ran to him and stared at the fear etched on Timmy's face. Duncan asked him what had happened. *He couldn't hold the rope tight—and didn't know why. His hands musta slipped.*

Timmy showed up at school on the first day of classes, using a cane—everyone's shock registered on their faces. He ranked high as an athlete, but now he didn't go outside for recess. Various kids volunteered to get lunch from the cafeteria and bring it to the classroom, saving him that long walk.

He was absent a lot, too.

Duncan didn't understand and didn't know how to help. They adjusted the way they played, getting closer so Timmy didn't have to work as hard...or they did things that didn't take a lot of effort. He wanted to be with his friend.

No brothers, sisters or extended family in their age range nearby. Just the two of them lived in the neighborhood.

The boys saw when Duncan's dog got hit by a car—they sobbed together.

Duncan sat with him after Timmy's first crush, when she said to Timmy's face that she liked someone else. That scar ran deep.

They went bowling together—swimming, bike riding and hiking up the small hill in their neighborhood.

Now it seemed like a mountain never to conquer again.

Without warning, something poked him in the back. Timmy wielded the crutch. Snapping out of the daydream, he thrust his hands in the air.

"I surrender!!!" Duncan shrieked. Timmy got him again—and down they went, laughing into the grass. They lay there for a moment, basking in the sun.

Duncan started, "Hey, you wanna help me move some mulch? You can sit and push it around as best you can... and I'll bring it over in the wheelbarrow."

"Sure!" Timmy craved to do something... no matter how little. He sat right where Duncan put him, adjusting his position and spreading it out. Not perfect, but it wasn't meant to be pristine—it just happened.

Timmy attacked his task using his crutch, combined with the rake on the ground next to him. Duncan grinned every time he brought a new wheelbarrow full over.

He was trying to bury Timmy, but Timmy kept up, at least for a little while. They laughed, grabbed handfuls and tossed mulch snowballs around. Timmy started to slow down... so Duncan slowed down as well.

Soon though, Timmy called him over. "Help me up," Tim said, weary from all the activity. Duncan's jaw clenched for a second and in the next second, he was helping his friend off the ground.

"I think I need to go lie down and rest... but thanks for letting me try, Dunc!"

McKenna witnessed it all from the kitchen window.

Her heart broke for the boys, but it never showed. Those were Timmy's tears in her eyes.

"Moooom, I'll be right back—going to walk him home!" Duncan yelled.

"Okay, Lad," McKenna replied.

"Bye, Miss Drummond!" Timmy yelled as he waved.

"Goodbye, Timothy. Say hello to your parents for me! Tell them I'll call soon."

"Sure will!" Timmy answered. He loved when she called him Timothy.

The lad calls me Miss Drummond, the least I can do is return the favor.

She watched from the window as the boys moved down the street—Duncan on one side, the crutch on the other.

"Puir wee scone." *Poor child indeed.* Tears started to roll down her freckled cheeks. "'Tis a sin he doesn't d'serve."

⸺◆⸺

Chapter Three

M cKENNA REACHED for a soft dishcloth and wiped her eyes and cheeks.

You emotional ninny, you know better than to question God's will. Have empathy—yes, but not sorrow. It's not the Drummond way.

Her memories trickled back to her, like a stream in the Highlands, so long ago.

The Drummond way. The Highlands. The hardship. The suffering.

The shame.

A girl of 18? In love with The Provost? Of a different clan? Impossible! Never to be!

But there he preached. Perfection. Outside at the Graham Village square, tending to his flock. The parents and children all congregated around him, listening raptly.

Ethan spoke with such conviction and passion. Not of fire and brimstone, but of love, caring and understanding. He bade his followers not to hate. It is a useless emotion as it solves nothing.

"Hate not unto the Drummonds. Embrace them," Ethan said with quiet resolve. "If they question your intent, answer them with your goodwill. If they suspect your motive, prove to them you have no desire to take from them. If they say they do not need your help, do so anyway."

Ethan paused, set his eyes on his parishioners and waited for a voice of disagreement. None came. They revered this man. They lived his words and wore them like protective armor.

Suddenly, the crowd started to murmur and turned towards McKenna. She didn't feel threatened. She had no fear. The Provost spoke words of solace, and she was drawn to the message. It was not a message on the lips of most men.

"Come, join us. All are welcome at our table," said the Provost.

His gentle reassurance pulled her in. She sat in an empty chair and listened. His voice floated, lilting and hypnotic. Driven by duty, anchored in faith—*and as handsome as an Angel could be.* McKenna's cheeks flushed and gave her away.

Ethan spoke to her after the service. In fact, all came to her and talked to her. How could this be? *I've been told my whole life these people are to be feared*—she contemplated—*but I have nothing but love for them.*

My clan doesn't speak this way. But in softer moments, alone with her Father, he professed not to understand the hatred of man. *It appears there are others who think this way.*

She visited often, and the villagers affectionately called her Kenna. Ethan took to whispering that term of endearment as well.

Ethan spoke softly to McKenna late one night, "I will come to you before your village. I will let them view the man, not the Standard. Put faith in me, I believe all to be good, no matter their clan. Either I will be lauded or shunned. God's Plan will be made known to all present... and I will accept His will, whatever it may be."

McKenna feared the worst for her love but placed her belief in him and his words. That trust and confidence gave him strength as he bade her farewell. She disappeared into the mist with only her lantern to guide her.

It felt like a whirlwind; it was perfect—until it wasn't.

A Drummond Clan member named Aswan witnessed her coming back from the Graham Village late that evening. Early the next day, he proclaimed in the Village Square that the Drummond's name had been soiled.

The men of the hamlet swore to take up arms. The womenfolk would punish her for her misdeeds.

In the Graham village, Ethan set forth as he promised, unaware of the maelstrom he would enter.

McKenna protested her innocence to all who came to judge... The crowd steadily grew. Women hissed and spat at her feet. The men gathered in a small group, plotting their revenge.

We can arrange raids! Burn their stored hay! Open their fence line and let loose their cattle!

The sound of hooves drew closer. Ethan circled the Village on his mount. He rode right to the clachan centre, where McKenna stood in judgement atop the large wooden dais.

Dismounting, his cape billowed beneath a gleaming breastplate. His warrior gauntlets beat against it, drawing attention from all present.

A silence fell on the group as he continued striking his chest. *Madness had overtaken him...* when he suddenly stopped, focused upon the crowd. He turned to meet

McKenna's gaze.

Ethan took her by the hand but spoke to those gathered.

His voice commanded them to listen.

"I come to you not to be your adversary. I come to defend this woman. She has done nothing for you to cast guilt towards her. She has done nothing to dishonor the great Drummond name," he thundered, their attention frozen.

"It is not for Man to judge who is right or wrong. The Almighty makes that decision when we go before him on our own Judgement Day."

"I come to your Elders this day to ask their acceptance of the Graham Clan as brothers under God, the way it is meant to be," Ethan continued.

Ethan turned to Lachlan Drummond. "This"—he swept his hand across the landscape—"is yer land. As guests, the Graham Clan came and sought safety from the hills. Both clans have learned to live together. I implore your kindness to let us remain in harmony."

He removed his warrior gloves, then peeled away the linen wraps beneath, baring his hands to the cold.

One hand pressed to the armor over his heart. The other reached toward the sky.

"If peace cannot be granted, then I place my faith in Dugald Graham to lead me beyond when you strike me down and spill my blood on the very earth he trod upon."

With one swift motion, he stripped the breastplate from his body and flung it to the ground. It landed with a sickening crash against the rocks and mud.

With steady breath, Ethan drew his sword—not to brandish it, but to offer it. He ran its edge across his palm. A thin ribbon of blood beaded along his skin. He planted the tip of the blade in the dirt.

Lachlan stared in silence. He searched the eyes of his fellow clan members. Weary men, willing to stand if needs be. Proud men.

Then he spotted a boy, young and innocent, looking towards McKenna, crying her name. They both had the arm wraps of the same family. The child dried his eyes on his sleeves then stood in defiance, as a Drummond male should.

This verity shall not be his verity—Lachlan's silent prayer lifted to the Heavens.

Then, with disdain, he removed his gloves, stripped his hands bare, and let the gauntlets fall to the ground. Armor no longer mattered.

Ethan reached up and placed the hilt in Lachlan's hand.

Ethan's hand touched Lachlan's briefly. Little did Lachlan know, Ethan had touched his heart as well.

Under their feet, the earth tasted Ethan's blood as it dripped from his hand.

And Ethan knelt.

The crowd held its breath. The wind stirred the Graham banner Ethan had planted, yet the Drummond standards stood still—heavy in the hush.

McKenna looked upon love, willing to surrender everything for what he believed in.

Lachlan stared down at the man before him, then at the sword.

A man pressed forth from the gathering towards Ethan. His steps were slow. His gaze pierced armor and cloth alike.

Alastair, brother to Aswan, the accuser, ranked as the most respected warrior in the Drummond Clan: a shrewd tactician, Master Archer and second to no one with the sword. A hawk was etched deep into his breastplate, signifying his cunning and lethality. He moved with uncertainty and with perplexed glances, fighting his own internal moral compass.

To witness him so unsure unsettled many present.

He approached and spoke with passion, "We have lore, 'ave been told the stories. My great-great-grandfather passed them to my great-grandfather, he passed it on to his son. My grandfather passed it to MY father. My father passed it to me."

"Every Drummond knows the Myth — we call him Dugald Albios."

"T'was generations ago that it was relayed by Kieran Drummond, a story passed down to us and guiding us to this daay."

"You call to the name of Dugald, but you bear witness that he be GRAHAM?"

Ethan did not look up. He would not move from his position of fealty.

"Aye, from my lips to any God who cares to hear my testimony. A Graham he is."

Gasps rippled across the crowd. Lachlan stared at the awe in his kinsman's eyes. The Clan Chief studied his men's faces, scarred over the years. Women clutched their children close with fear. The breeze stirred the leaves, not crushed into the mud by soggy feet. Alastair and Lachlan glanced at each other, bewildered.

His gaze lowered to the hilt, a simple blue jewel affixed to its pommel, the grip wrapped in deep forest green twine. Lachlan, unsure, gripped it with both bare hands and lifted the weapon above his head.

He appeared ready to strike, but instead, snapped the edge onto his unprotected, weathered palms and drew it across his own hand.

He dropped to one knee and proclaimed for all to hear, "The stories passed down to me, etched into my soul, but I never believed it to be true. And now, a man comes, and... I.." Lachlan choked on his words.

"I've never seen a man as pure and full of love until this very moment." His gaze locked on the man before him—Ethan's head still bowed to accept his fate. "Rise and have no fear of me."

Lachlan stood, grasping Ethan in the traditional warrior's clasp, known to those who have stood in battle.

Lachlan pleaded, "Provost Graham, it is my most reverent request that you minister to Clan Drummond as you tend to Clan Graham—your word is true and intentions are pure." He looked directly at Aswan, "Many are in need of light and goodness."

A collective breath left everyone present, McKenna included. She could love Ethan the man, while honoring her name and the man who brought peace to the Valley that day. Little did they realize there were Dark Forces yet to come.

The Provost left the village, and McKenna continued with her life, visiting both villages with Ethan, as his consort. As Fall wilted to Winter, she showed that she was with child—but not yet wed.

She dared not soil his name, so she requested Ethan to secrete her away to a village some distance from Lochlane. The Provost made sure no harm came to pass, but the Graham Midwife feared the worst.

T hey were a long way from proper care. She began having difficulty with the pregnancy... shortly followed by false labour pains. Her bed, which was harsh, uncomfortable, and yet unavoidable, confined her to an unjust cage.

The Midwife pleaded, "Kenna, lass, I fear for you and The Provost's issue. I have great fear for you both!"

The Midwife summoned The Provost, who came to McKenna's side and stayed with her for two weeks' time. Her agony was almost too much to bear, but he was always present to calm her. His gentle touch soothed and steadied her.

The Midwife confided her fear—the baby may be an Angel in the breeze before a Child of the earth.

McKenna showed no outward sign of her distress. She swore Ethan would not bear any encumbrance. *He offered to die for me; I shall not shame him with a lack of courage.*

In private, she wept and prayed for God to intervene and take her burden.

Then, one day, the baby moved, and with it came a calm unlike any she could recall. No more pain. No more fear.

Her apprehension disappeared. She called out for Ethan.

He came from outside, but before he could mount the stairs, McKenna birthed a boy, complete in every way. Kenna had no pain, no cries in labour, indeed, no difficulty at all.

She counted fingers and toes, made sure the limbs were whole and strong. The child had a wonderful dark complexion and a tuft of reddish-brown hair. He did not cry; he did not squirm. He had an awareness that she had never seen.

And in the door, The Provost witnessed his progeny. Perfect, healthy and alive.

The Midwife, herself clad in Graham Tartan, took the child, cleaned him up and presented him back to McKenna, swaddled in a Drummond cloth and wrapped in a Graham Tartan blanket.

She said to McKenna, "M'Lady, your bairn... of both Clans."

The Provost looked on with pride, as well as sadness. He realized what this birth meant for his young love. Shame, ridicule and judgment would follow her, unjustly. He would not stand for that, for his Kenna.

After several days, Ethan confided in his son's mother. The stories and hopes they had shared in confidence, now threatened to haunt them in love.

The weight of her past pulled at the very core of the Unity they had both hoped for. He swore to send her to safety, to live in peace, away from judgment, removed from the scandal. Ethan Graham took his oath; she would be given the means to survive and thrive.

McKenna wept, but understood the implications of what faced them.

She affixed her eyes on Ethan, his gaze thick with the tragedy he must carry by this choice. Her face was lined with sorrow, but steeled by the duty she must now face.

Words between them would have been as hollow as a bell without a striker.

With a gentle kiss on his hand and a caress of her cheek, she turned him towards the door and bade the man she loved farewell.

The room quieted. Ethan's footsteps faded away. Soon, the hoof falls of his horse faded into nothingness. McKenna faced solitude borne of love and devotion.

The Graham Midwife appeared carrying a bathing vessel. She took her time, cleaning the streaks of tears on McKenna's face with the soft cloth. She held the new mother close, providing some comfort in the empty and barren room.

She asked, "What will you call him, Mu'um?"

McKenna answered with purpose, "This is Duncan—'Tis my little dark warrior."

A voice called out, breaking her dream.

McKenna focused her eyes. Duncan was returning from Timmy's house. She met him at the side kitchen door when it opened.

With cookies.

Chapter Four

T HE ANDERSON HOUSE was not your typical suburban home. Outside, there was a beautiful walkway, edged with a flower bed. Every morning, the sprinkler would come on and soak the flowers—and the walkway.

On sunny mornings, a faint rainbow shimmered through the misting water, punctuated by wildflowers of every color and kind.

Overflowing pots of petunias hung from the porch, contrasting with the pale green siding of the house and brick-lined windows. Blair adored her flora, and the outside reminded her of her Grandmother's house, a world away.

She had only seen pictures of it, but she loved how it looked and how it blended with the surrounding landscape. Donald made sure it had everything she asked for. He appreciated it was her domain and let her have it, with pride.

This continued until Christmas, when it was his turn.

Donald was the Commander of the Decorations. In the summer, it was the colors of the flowers; in the winter, it was the glow of the lights.

It was the toast of the town and earned write-ups in the local paper. "Better Homes and Gardens hasn't visited us yet," Blair stated with a coy wink, many times.

When you walked through the front door, you expected that same comforting touch, but now, it was nowhere to be found.

Furniture had been moved to make wider walkways. Support rails were randomly placed around the halls. Chairs were at different heights. A ramp was on the side of the house, but one had to search for it. Out back, the swing set was being battered by Mother Nature. It hadn't been used for some time. Usually, it was covered for the winter, but not now. No one bothered to maintain it...

B lair spied the boys coming down the street. Duncan was whistling. They were both in good spirits. It warmed her to see them like this. These memories crowded out others too painful to recall.

Once they got to the door, Blair opened it wide. The friends wedged themselves through and stepped in. Duncan made sure Timmy was steady, then grabbed the walker. He leaned on it and shifted his weight off the crutch, so Duncan took it and leaned it near the door.

"It's right here, ready for you!" Duncan exclaimed.

Timmy wore his exhaustion like a heavy coat, but he mustered a smile for his friend. "Thanks Dunc. Maybe we'll see each other tomorrow, okay?" he said, catching his breath.

Duncan could tell how run-down he was, but didn't let on. He patted Timmy's shoulder and shifted his gaze up to Blair.

"My Mom's gonna call you soon, Mrs. Anderson!" relayed Duncan.

Blair answered with a heavy sigh, "You tell her to do that, Child. Now off with you."

With a wave, Duncan was off, back up the street. Timmy stared after him. Once Duncan was out of sight, Timmy's head drooped.

"We wrestled some, then he put me to work, spreading some mulch. It was fun." A long pause weighed down his following words. "I wish I could have more fun..." His voice trailed off.

"No wonder you are so exhausted!" she exclaimed. "Let's clean you up a bit so you can lie down until it's time for dinner."

"Okay, Mom, but I'm just gonna go to bed. I'm really tired," Timmy said in defeat. He always needed help now. He hated it. Even as his mother washed his face, he hated he couldn't do it himself.

It felt like some mysterious monster was coming in at night, stealing little bits and pieces of him in secret. It wasn't fair. His blood boiled just under the surface.

But he never let on to his mother. Timmy could be vulnerable with his father—but nothing but strength in front of his mother. Donald recognized what was happening. He was being robbed of his son. The last thing he wanted to have happen was for Blair to think it was her fault.

Years ago, Blair and Donald came here to the edge of the James River. It reminded them so much of the rivers back home, Blair begged the man she loved to find them a house along its peaceful banks.

"So much like Gran's!" she told Donald.

So, he searched and searched, but nothing was already built anywhere nearby. He didn't let that deter him. He found a parcel of unkempt land, purchased the lot and started clearing it himself.

Nestled alongside the river's edge, with a glorious view of the rushing water—he couldn't ask for a better place to settle.

One day, while clearing the field, the neighboring landowner approached him. He'd recently sold his parcel to a developer planning a new neighborhood. The property line ran directly through Donald's intended driveway. The developer occasionally stopped by to make a few suggestions to an appreciative Donald.

A flurry of activity followed. In the end, the developer had done most of the prep work—and may have helped Donald a bit, to keep his 'neighbor' happy.

Donald got nearly all the work done on the new place for pennies on the dollar. The developer and builders realized that every prospective buyer would pass Donald's house on the way in—it only made sense to give it curb appeal to sell the dream neighborhood beyond.

One day, unbeknownst to Blair, they took a drive through a 'new' subdivision along the river. She took in the parcel of land, the landscaping, and the burgeoning neighborhood beyond.

She'd had enough of apartment living, and now she knew exactly what she wanted.

She begged him to stop. Climbing out of the car, she took in the scene—then turned to him with eyes full of hope and whispered, "This is the kind of thing I want for us."

Donald walked around the vehicle, surveyed the eyes of the woman he cherished for years, and said, "Then, love, let it be yours." He held out his hand—the keys glistening in the sun.

"What did you say?" she asked, hardly believing his words.

"This is the place of your dreams," he said with pride, "but it's as real as you or I."

"Then let's plant our family stake," Blair said. She laid her head on Donald's shoulder and thanked the Heavens for a man such as he.

Blair stood outside, looking at her postcard-perfect house. So many things came to pass—and so fast!

Families began moving in down the street. They all stopped by, talking about the beauty of the subdivision—and the house that led you into such a peaceful scene. Blair loved being the neighborhood matriarch, though she was the same age as most of the other women.

Backyard cookouts, baking exchanges, and flower clubs for the women. The men? They stood around bragging about their new lawn mowers, the latest driveway repair, or playing lumberjack on some poor tree felled by the last winter storm.

Then came the kids, as if it had been scripted. First Jean, then Donna, followed by Ally.

It MUST be something in the water. An inside joke only the neighborhood ladies shared. The neighborhood men? Clueless.

And then it happened to Blair. The whole neighborhood was in on her pregnancy. Everyone had to have details.

When are you due?
Do you want a boy or a girl?
Imagine growing up in that paradise!

On the day of her shower, she didn't know she had so many neighbors. They just kept coming—and the pile of gifts nearly didn't fit in the nursery! Planning, packing, cooking and food prep were a group effort. Blair didn't have to lift a finger!

And when labor started? It was like an alarm went off in the development. A stream of cars followed the two of them to the hospital. The waiting room was so full, nurses had trouble getting through to the ward.

That's how beloved she was.

The actual birth?

That was a celebration in the whole community. Timothy was the Prince of James Bend. The couple couldn't believe their good fortune.

As he grew up, the neighborhood slowed down and settled into an idyllic pace.

The frenzy gave way to parental responsibilities—lots of babysitting. One couple would go about their normal activities for a night, while another minded the fort. Carpools formed: daycare in the morning, kindergarten in the afternoon.

Families aged, and as time wilted away, many moved on. New ones came to replace them, but it wasn't the same.

The entire community grew up together.

And now, that time was a fleeting memory.

E arly one summer day, Blair was outside, watering her beloved flowers, when a car went by. Being a redhead herself, her radar was up when other fiery locks went by.

Three doors down, a head full of Rohan tresses stepped out of an older, beat-up sedan, surveying the house next to where they pulled in. A young boy bounced out of the passenger side, ran onto the lawn and squealed, "Mumma! Is this it? Is this where we are going to move?"

"Yes, lad," McKenna mussed Duncan's hair as he whizzed by.

Blair's ears perked up. *Couldn't be.*

Before the thought faded, her own boy darted past her, running straight at the strangers.

"Haaay! My name is Timmy! I live up the street!"

"Timothy, what a grand name! My name is McKenna Drummond, and that rolling on the ground is m' boy Duncan."

Blair's heart swelled. *Another Scot?* Living this close? She set down the watering can and walked toward McKenna.

"Dunc? *YOU* can't catch me!" Timmy teased.

"Oh, yes, I can!" Duncan replied, launching into a full-speed chase into the backyard.

As Blair approached the driveway, she scuffed a rock on the road. McKenna turned towards the sound, and seeing another redhead gave her reason to smile.

"Dia Dhuit, lass," Blair said, a traditional greeting from The Highlands, testing the waters.

McKenna's mouth fell open. Her native tongue had been missing for years. Her eyes welled up as she stepped forward and embraced Blair like a long-lost cousin.

"Dia Dhuit," she whispered in Blair's ear.

The embrace between the two warmed corners of their souls that had been quiet—and cold—for far too many years.

The rest of that summer was a blur of action. Painting, cleaning, moving and collapsing after lengthy days. Timmy and Duncan were real warriors, carrying the boxes in, taking them to the right rooms, then crashing down the stairs for the next trip. Timmy even went with them to McKenna's small apartment to help pack.

The boys threw things in crates as fast as they could, but McKenna would tell them to do it slower—then show them how.

Timmy would always answer, "Yes, Ma'am." His manners sat front and center. Duncan started to imitate him. "Yes, Ma'am," he would say, trying to sound like his friend.

When the snacks came out, they might have forgotten to be as polite, but she didn't care. Her boy had been without a friend for years, so her heart was light when she saw the two of them together.

"Okay, lads, we have to go!" McKenna would holler in the small hallway.

Cue the testosterone tempest.

On one such moving day, as they pulled up, McKenna squinted and thought she was at the wrong house. Something didn't seem right. Blair popped up, a spade in her hand, her hair in a fiery red swirling ponytail and sweat on her brow.

"My gift to you," Blair stated. She stood behind McKenna and placed her arms around her neck and shoulders. McKenna reached for her arms with both hands. "You need some color in front of your house, so I took some of mine and transplanted them here. Git you right started in y'er new place."

McKenna gazed at the beauty her friend surgically placed in the front yard.

"Aye. We din'nt have such appointments in the Village where I am from. 'Tis a pleasure to behold. I can'nt thank you enough, lass," McKenna said, a smile across her face.

"No need to thank me." Blair waved her off. McKenna reeled at the palette of colors laid before her.

Blair spoke up, "We just be a couple of Gingers..."—*not in a bad way*—she paused and smiled, "...watching o'er flowers and boys..." She leaned in and whispered, "...and the men get the gift of watchi' a couple 'o lookers like us!"

Blair had a lilt to her voice that was hard to resist.

"So'os let 'em—" The two laughed, a little giddy.

"Now I'm fixin' for a spot. Join me, *Piuthar*?"

To hear the word 'sister' in her own language tugged at Blair in ways she couldn't explain.

They leaned in, closed their eyes and pressed their foreheads together in unity... then left the kids in the yard and wandered inside for refreshments.

For the rest of the summer, McKenna met the other women in the neighborhood—but she was in Blair's orbit, and she liked it. The others pulled back a bit. They sensed it wasn't about the hair. It was something more profound. Heritage. You couldn't break it.

Timmy and Duncan were the same. Plenty of kids around, but those two were inseparable.

Grass needs mowing? They tackled it. Downspout clogged? They were in it, elbows deep. Hauling river stone to build a wall? Two can do it faster than one.

They played ball. They organized races down the block. They went fishing—Timmy hated baiting his hook, so Duncan did it for him. Duncan always caught the bigger fish, but somehow... it was always smaller when they showed their moms.

One year, Timmy repeated a grade because of some poor marks, but now he was in Duncan's class—and Duncan took to tutoring him with glee. He got to be the one in charge, even if only to teach for an hour a week.

Blair remarked to McKenna one night, "I think m'boy might've stayed back on purpose—just to be in Duncan's class. That's whut I think."

McKenna nodded. "I wouldn't put it past them." Those boys were always up to something.

That year, the boys were on every local sports team—football, basketball, baseball—and still found time to tear around the neighborhood playing all sorts of made-up games.

Red Light, Green Light, but with a twist: You had to make it from one tree to another during the count—or else. And blindfolded dodgeball? Once the blindfold went on, everyone had to freeze in place and pray the thrower didn't have Spidey sense.

Many a garden—and more than a few fences—were innocent casualties of those games, to be sure.

Blair and McKenna would view their shenanigans from a porch. You'd always eye one head on the other's shoulder, but it didn't matter which.

For Timmy, little physical things started in that year.

Duncan was getting faster in foot races and winning more street games. It didn't seem like much at first—just growth spurts. McKenna and Blair would often comment on how Duncan was growing up so fast.

But Timothy saw something else.

He noticed that he couldn't grip the ball some days. Or how his leg would sting when he ran—like that pins-and-needles feeling when your foot falls asleep, but without the pins. All over weakness.

Sometimes he'd wake up in the middle of the night, sweating for no reason. Or he'd stay home from school with a fever. At first, it seemed like a phase. But spring turned into summer, and it didn't pass.

Blair, ever stubborn, gave up the notion of 'growing pains' and took Timmy to the pediatrician.

Timmy tried to dodge the questions like boys do at the doctor's. He wasn't sick—he was tired. A long week of practice. He could still beat Duncan in most things.

Most things he said.

That phrase stuck with Blair.

They were in the same grade... but he was nearly a year

and a half older.

That's odd.

They scheduled a follow-up. Blair told the doctor she'd bring her husband next time. Tests would be run—to rule things out. The doctor didn't seem concerned. The nurse? Furiously scribbling notes behind the counter, out of Blair's view.

That night, Blair told McKenna about the appointment, about the follow-up and Donald would be coming. She couldn't remember if bringing him was her idea—or the doctor's.

"I'm sure t'weren't anything," Blair said, her voice faltering. "If it were something, they'd've kept us. True, lass?"

"Aye," McKenna said.

She smiled, stroked Blair's cheek, then patted her knee.

Brave face, for her. McKenna drifted back to Ethan's calming touch during her own difficult pregnancy—and tried to give Blair the same comfort now.

T he following week, Donald, Blair, and Timmy went back to the doctor. They had already done the at-home specimen collection and brought it by. That was a thing Timmy never wanted to do again.

"A poop sample? Why, Ma? Eww."

But that was in the past. Timmy was never going to do that again. No sir.

They arrived at the office, checked in and were shown into a waiting conference room. Not an examining room.

An office, where charts and anatomical posters lined the walls. A whiteboard was on one side, windows on the other. Timmy walked over and stared outside. He did not want to be in this strange place. It was the beginning of summer. He wanted to go swimming in the river, maybe go fishing. Anywhere but here.

Timmy felt good. He told his parents that morning that he felt good. What he didn't tell them was that he had to change his pajamas because his sweat had soaked through them.

Twice.

The door to the room swung open. The nurse came in with a very official and stern look. Glancing down at the chart, she inquired with a somber, solemn tone, "Are YOU Timmy Anderson? According to this chart, you have a problem." A pause hung in the air, and Timmy gulped.

"Says here you..." she glanced up over the rim of her glasses. "... LIKE LOLLIPOPS?" She grinned at Timmy. She was no longer the enemy.

"Do I?" Timmy exclaimed.

"Follow me and we will go find one," the nurse said. They left the room. Things were looking good. Timmy got to the nurses' station—some were standing around. They all knew Timmy's name, and he didn't think anything of it.

They all understood.
A conversation was going on with his parents.
And now, it was common knowledge.

Timmy picked a sour lemon lollipop. He liked them because *nobody* took those, so he always had a choice.

The nurse brought him back to the office where his parents were. They walked in, The doctor was sitting down. Papers filled the conference table. His parents were on the other side.

His mom was crying.

A ll those memories rushed back into Blair's mind as she helped Timmy wash up. He appeared like a shadow of the boy who stood in that doctor's office months ago.

"Let's go, into bed, lad," she whispered. They moved across the hall. They had moved the bedroom to the first floor to make nighttime trips to the bathroom easier.

Blair and Donald slept in the small den downstairs to be close to him. The upstairs bedrooms had remained unused for months. Once the cane made its appearance, everything changed.

Rooms shifted. Furniture was shoved aside to create wider walking paths. Toys that once filled every corner were now tucked away. The ramp at the back of the house arrived one weekend when everyone came together for Blair's family.

Refrigerator art had been carefully removed and put away. She couldn't look at the drawings Timmy made, where he had a crutch or a cane in them.

Just as Blair had done for the community over the years, they returned the favor. They rallied around her, as neighbors do.

Leading the charge was McKenna.

No one endured it more than she did. McKenna, who had not been meant to carry a child, had been given a miracle. And now Blair, who experienced the joy of motherhood, faced the unthinkable possibility of losing hers.

Blair helped Timmy into bed. She leaned in to kiss his forehead.

"G'night, my love. Tomorrow morning—special treat! Pancakes. Chocolate or blueberry?" she asked, slipping into full Mother mode.

"I'll pick tomorrow, okay? I'm tired." Timmy said with a heavy breath. "Love you, Mum." He forced a brave smile for his mom. She rose from the bed and stepped into the hall.

One last glance back—Timmy couldn't view the doorway from where he lay, but she saw everything. Blair studied for a moment, his chest rising and falling—slow, steady.

In the depths of summer, Timmy's days were growing shorter.

Blair turned and headed down the hallway. She stopped at the entrance to the kitchen. The emotions caught up to her, and her tears started to flow. She ached for Donald. She wept for herself. She sobbed for Timmy.

She grabbed the door frame with both hands, trying to stay standing, but failed. She slid down the doorframe into a heap on the floor.

Her sobbing found its way into her bones. Every fiber within her ached alongside her heart.

Thank God Timmy can't see me. She buried her face in her hands.

In Timmy's room, his cheeks carried tears down his own face. He didn't need to see.

He heard.

After a lifetime on the floor, Blair pulled herself up and reached for the phone. She dialed a number.

"*Piuthar,* I need you. Can you come over at nine a.m.?"

The next morning, McKenna stood at her front door.

She held a tray of muffins—still warm. She had lain awake all night. Blair's voice triggered something deep inside her. She didn't know what was wrong. She didn't need to.

She just accepted: They would face it together.

Duncan sensed something wasn't right. His mother

was in her own world. She didn't respond to his "Good morning!" when he walked into the kitchen. He grasped that the muffins she was baking weren't for them.

She told him to dress on his own—that she had to meet Blair about something, and that he was to entertain himself for a couple of hours. She'd be back soon. But behave.

Then out the front door she went, and up the street.

Duncan sensed he shouldn't—but he slipped out the side door, still in his pajamas, and followed her to Timmy's house. He wandered up next to his mother. She felt him beside her, and she reached down, patting the back of his head.

He knew he'd done the right thing. Before she touched the doorbell, the door flew open.

Blair stood before them, disheveled. Duncan was startled, so he hid behind his mother. Blair tried to speak. Her lips moved, but nothing came out.

"What is it, lass?" pleaded McKenna. She stepped forward as Blair stepped back. McKenna placed the muffin tin on the small end table and reached for Blair's hand.

"I'm here. Tell me."

"Timmy has the Polio," Blair blurted. She began to

weep again, collapsing into McKenna's arms. "I... I should have told you sooner, but..."

"He... he couldn't get out... of the bed this morning. I... I waited too long... I..."

Her voice broke apart under the weight of her grief. McKenna held her close, arms wrapped tightly around her.

The women sank into the couch. McKenna clung to Blair the way the Graham Midwife once clung to her, so many years ago. She needed to be there. Nothing more.

Duncan had been forgotten. He stood inside the door alone. The women were on the couch, engaged in something he didn't understand. It was confusing and unclear. Duncan hadn't been this far into Timmy's house in a long time.

It looked... different. It wasn't messy, just cluttered—like nothing was quite where it should be.

Timmy's room was upstairs, but something pulled him down the hallway. He didn't understand it, but he didn't ignore it.

A bed sat in the room on the left... and Duncan stepped in. He focused on Timmy lying on his back. His eyes were open—but hollow.

"Heeey," Duncan greeted him, the usual way.

Timmy didn't respond right away. Eventually, his head turned toward Duncan.

"I'm so tired, Dunc," he whispered.

"Did I tire you out yesterday? Did we do too much?" Duncan asked, the guilt already flooding in. Maybe they did too much. Perhaps he shouldn't have made Timmy wrestle.

Maybe he—

"No, no, no," Timmy cut him off weakly. "You didn't do anything."

Duncan's world was collapsing. "You're my best friend. I'm so sorry if I... if I did something... if I made you—"

His speech faltered.

"Dunc, this isn't you," Timmy said, trying to sound firm. "I'm just sick."

Duncan broke. His mother wasn't there to hold him. And he didn't want to cry—but he couldn't help it.

"Dunc, I can barely move."

Duncan was weeping now, overcome with something he couldn't understand at his early age. "I'm so sorry. I'm so sorry."

Something pulled him closer.

Duncan reached out, trembling, and rested his hands on Timmy's shoulders.

"Dunc, don't... I—"

That syllable stuck.

The room filled with light.

"Timothy Anderson, you get up out of that bed RIGHT NOW!"

Duncan's voice cracked through the brightness, startling Timmy.

The light vanished.

And Timmy was *on his feet*.

His arms were wrapped around Duncan, holding him as he cried.

Timmy... was standing.

He held Duncan up and steadied his friend's legs. Together, they walked into the hallway. Timmy saw his Mom, Dad, and Miss Drummond talking in the living room.

They'll know what to do.

They stepped through the doorway. "Help!" Timmy called out.

"I don't know what's wrong with Dunc!"

The room went silent. Three adults stared in disbelief. Confusion gave way to action.

They rushed to the boys.

———————◆———————

Chapter Five

S HE TOOK DUNCAN home that night. He was not his usual self. He couldn't describe how he felt other than that he was sore all over. After a day or so, his personality seemed to appear out of nowhere.

That night, McKenna kept to herself. She had never spoken of Duncan's birth... how easy it was or how Ethan calmed her with the touch of his hand. More-so, how the lore that had been passed down throughout her clan contained mysteries she never quite grasped. And now, another mystery presented itself.

The entire summer came and went. Timmy was getting stronger. The doctors couldn't understand it. No matter what tests they ran, nothing pointed to a clinical explanation. Blair and Donald were beside themselves. Their world was crashing down before them, and in an instant, everything was right again.

One morning in the early fall, McKenna asked her son about that night.

"Duncan, that morning, why d'yeh follow me?" she

inquired.

"I don't know. I saw you walking up the street and wanted to go with you." Duncan replied between sips of his chocolate milk. To him, it was just another day.

"Lad, you know Timmy was very sick. Y'did know it?" McKenna was still puzzled.

"It was bad, bad, horrible. I... I might have hurt him when we played that day..." Duncan started, "...but Timmy said it wasn't my fault."

Duncan took a deep breath and continued. "I felt so bad, I wanted him to not be sick. Next thing I know, I went to hug him, but I ended up yelling. I don't remember what I said or why..." Duncan's voice trailed off. He shouted at Timmy. *Not good. Not good at all.*

After a long silence, Duncan told his mother, "Then, we were standing in the living room and Timmy was holding me up." He turned to his mother with a confused look.

"What happened?" he asked, eyes searching his mother's face.

McKenna struggled to recount the details in a way her boy would understand. Searching the patterns on the rug, she found no secrets or answers hidden there. She started, "We were in the living room. Mrs. Anderson and I were talking, and she was crying. She was so upset."

She continued, "Mr. Anderson came home and sat down with us, and we talked more," she said, combing her memory.

"A light bulb in the corridor, I think, got really bright and then faded out. The three of us stopped talking for a minute, then started again."

She finished, "The next thing I recall... You and Timmy were standing in the hallway."

It made no sense to Duncan. "A bulb burned out?" *Was that the light I saw?*

"The thing was, the light was on when we collected the two of you, so I've nary an idea of what we saw..." McKenna was trying to make sense of it all herself.

He was curious. "When I yelled at Timmy, I remember seeing a bright glow too. But it was really close to us, not in the hallway. I was on the other side of his bed."

Duncan's face froze. Something triggered a memory. He wasn't afraid, but he didn't understand.

Duncan blurted out, "My hands got warm right then... and they tingled. Like when you give somebody a shock, but it lasted a lot longer."

McKenna's eyes opened wide in disbelief.

Her own memories came flooding back. Ethan—when she was pregnant—all those times he calmed her? Or at Duncan's birth? Just before—when he moved—she experienced no pain? No distress during birth?

All she remembered was a wave of warmth passing over her. The warmth shut out the pain, the worry and the concern. The outside world melted away and disappeared.

All those times she'd be crying, missing her Ethan... and Duncan, as a small boy, would crawl into her lap. And the warmth would wash over her.

She bit her tongue in front of him. Her mind was a jumble, and she had no idea how to ask the boy or to tell him some of her memories. She had always talked of Ethan as a brave and honest man who loved them very much and would join them when the time was right.

I don't want to confuse the lad more. McKenna sighed as she went quiet.

So, breakfast came and went. The boys played in the backyard—the morning's events were long forgotten.

After dinner, they searched for something on nighttime TV. Duncan wanted something funny. Sunday night, 'Wonderful World Of Disney' was on, so they got their popcorn and plopped in front of the tube.

It so happened that the episode was full of cartoons.

'Donald Duck' was his favorite. "He's like Mr. Anderson, the same name." Duncan said out loud and laughed. "It's almost like mine, too," Duncan mentioned in passing.

" 'Tis, almost," McKenna replied. He had such an active imagination, and McKenna loved it when he was lost in thought, wondering out loud. She loved listening to all the questions and ideas he came up with, even the silly ones—her mind wandered for a second when Duncan brought her back to reality.

"...it's almost the same spelling!" Duncan exclaimed.

McKenna, bewildered, paused for a moment. Then she prodded, "The same as what?"

"Dugald," he said matter-of-factly.

McKenna drew back, surprised, and looked at the boy in front of her. How would he know that name? She had never spoken about the lore of her land before.

"I bet they are related. I bet we are all related cause we spell our names almost the same." Duncan was too busy watching the cartoon to see how perplexed her stare was.

Her head tilted, red hair cascaded over her shoulder. "From where d'you hear that name?"

"I dreamed it one night. It was scary at first cause I was outside alone, but it told me things were okay and I shouldn't be afraid. So I wasn't." He relayed the dream with such detail that it unnerved her.

"What else did it say?" As soon as she spoke, she regretted asking.

"It said, 'Go to your friend', and we did the next day," he said, still watching the cartoons. "He talks like you and Mrs. Anderson," he paused for a moment, then, "I've had a lot of dreams about Timmy and the things we did."

Duncan had no fear, no concern or worry in his voice. He didn't question these dreams and had never mentioned them before.

Could...Could it be? McKenna asked herself, and she pulled him closer. Suddenly, it overcame her.

The warmth washed over her. In her heart, she knew instantly. *Did the lore pass to her boy?*

M onths later, on a rainy afternoon, Duncan thumbed through a book in his room. He loved reading about history and different people moving around. He was fascinated by how nomadic tribes would move from one place to another to find better places to live, hunt for food, and make life easier.

Duncan loved reading about the Wild West. He read about how pioneers moved westward into inhospitable lands and learned to live with the fierce animals and the people who were already living on the plains or mountains.

He never understood how one group would push another out. Why did they always fight? *It's not like there wasn't enough space for all of them.* He loved the stories of cattle and tending the herds.

"It was like that back where I am from… even earlier, according to some books I've read," McKenna said from her boy's bedroom doorway.

"We used to have groups of people called clans, and they would always fight and not trust one another. They didn't like each other very much," she continued.

Duncan was sitting up on his bed listening with interest.

"Your father and I were part of different clans. He was a Graham, and I was a Drummond. Back then, those clans didn't get along—but sometimes they would cooperate, like in a hard winter, they would share food, or in bad storms, both would dam up the river so it wouldn't flood the valley we shared."

McKenna's voice was wistful and dreamy, and Duncan listened raptly.

"I visited the Graham village once to fetch some feed one Spring, and that's where I met your father. He was a handsome and righteous man. I imagine he still is. He helped to heal the wounds of our clans and make us strong, as One, under God."

"He was the bravest man you'd ever meet. And you, my lil Duncan, are brave and handsome like him!"

"Am I like him, Mum? Do I look like him? I am not afraid of anything, just like him!"

McKenna swelled with pride.

Her little dark warrior was very much like Ethan.

"Aye, boy, indeed yer Father wasn't afraid of anything. But he worried for us. He didn't think, at first, that the Clans would get along, so he sent us away to protect us. He protects us to this very day. What we have is because of him and the help he sends us often."

She looked back on her past with Ethan, and the Clans.

"You are so much like him. You have the Graham kinship in you. You care for everybody before yourself, and I am sure he'd be right proud of you."

She continued, "The Drummond name goes back for centuries. But so does Graham. We have folklore about that name and the things they have done for their fellow man. All of the clans remember them and speak of the things they did."

"D' you remember who you mentioned to me a little while ago?" She inquired.

"Dugald," he answered without taking a breath.

She was caught off guard that he remembered, but continued on, "His is a name that endured for generations. People talk of his goodness and how he tended people he didn't know. He helped people, not expecting anything back."

"When I hear that name in my dreams, I am never afraid. I bet my Dad wasn't either!" Duncan was relaying facts as he understood them.

"How do you know your Father dreamed about him?" She asked with curiosity.

"Everyone dreams about Dugald...most people forget."

Duncan's innocence struck McKenna. A mere boy who understands so simply that all have the dream, but few remember it. She thought back to the lore she had heard all her life, back in the Drummond village.

"A long time ago," she recounted, "it is said that Dugald healed a young Drummond clan boy. He was very sick, but Dugald helped him. 'Twas a mystery, that."

"Even though he was from a different clan?" Duncan asked, but he wasn't curious. He just wanted the facts.

"Aye. No one knows where he caame from or where he went. They don't even knoow how he did it."

"Yer father did the same thing. Helped people, no maatter what their clan was."

"He helped me when I was sick. Do you understand, boy?" Duncan nodded.

"Many times when we all need help and someone comes along, and for whaatever reason, they are able to help."

"At times, you help too. Sometimes when I am sad, you come over and cuddle with me, and I feel better— it just 'appens. And, other times..."

Duncan cut her off, "Did.. Did.." Duncan was wrestling with the right words. McKenna had reason to pause.

"Aye. You helped Timmy, lad. I dun'na know how and what you did, but it's the only thing that makes sense."

"I know you're confused; we all are, but it is something that happened and nothing bad came of it. I dun'na know if it will ever happen again; 'tis important is that you know YOU had a purpose to do it. Don't be afraid of it or whatever Dugald or your Father were able to do..." McKenna drew a deep breath before she finished, "... but yoou might have their same gift."

McKenna eyed her boy. His head hung low. He breathed deep and lifted his head.

Gazing into her eyes, he said, "I understand now, Mumma."

His expression changed. Once questioning and searching, his eyes were now filled with passion and resolve.

McKenna looked upon her boy differently now. Reverence was the closest thing to describing it.

Soon, the conversation of that rainy day was long gone. Replaced by blustery snows, cold weather, snowmen and too much time indoors. Duncan hated winter.

He wanted to be outside.

He hated to stack layers; sweaters and jackets and mittens and hats. And the boots. Don't forget the boots. You had to put those on in the right order with everything else, or you couldn't bend over to buckle them. Only after all that do you get to go out.

And after getting battered by the snow and wind?

You had to take it all off again. And they never made it back to the hangar, or the hat and storage box. Well, not exactly. They made it back to the right places only when everything was soaking wet.

Duncan was taking off his boots. Plop! Plop! On the floor they went. Next, the snow jacket. Plop! Right next to the boots.

I'll pick everything up later. Duncan stared at the mess.

Now the snow pants. He undid them carefully as the zipper would catch on one side. Duncan stumbled on one of the boots on the floor and almost fell over. He wasn't paying attention.

The zipper grabbed some skin on his forearm and gave it a good scratch.

"Owww," Duncan yelled. He stared for a moment, there it was—a little blood. He hurried to finish getting undressed and ran right to the kitchen. He grabbed a paper towel and patted the scratch.

He peeked under the towel.

Mmm, not too bad, just a little one. He picked up his clothes and put them in their proper place.

McKenna yelled from the basement, "Are you alright? What did y'doo?"

He answered, "I scratched myself. I'm fine."

McKenna yelled back to her son, "Dun'na you bleed o'er everything or else I'll bleed y'myself!"

Gee, thanks, Ma. I'm dying with a mortal wound up here, and you don't want me to bleed on the carpet. Thanks a lot. Duncan sometimes was a little too fresh for his own good.

He stared at the drop of blood on his forearm.

He cocked his head and stared at his hands.

Wait. Could I—He glanced around to see if anyone was watching.

He placed his hand over the scratch. After a minute, he lifted his palm and peeked underneath.

Nope. Still bleeding. He wrinkled his nose, frustrated, and tried again. He closed his eyes and concentrated.

He inspected his arm. He shook his hands, trying to make them work.

Nothing.

Maybe he needs to think of Dugald or his Father. He shut his eyes again and put his hand over the scratch.

Still nothing.

He squinted at his arm. *Well, this is dumb.* He tossed his arms in the air.

McKenna had snuck up and was peering around the door. She watched it unfold before her eyes. She walked in, stroked his hair, got down on a knee, face to face with him.

"I dun'na think you choose when it 'appens, M'thinks IT chooses the when."

———————◆O◆———————

Chapter Six

D<small>UNCAN STROLLED THROUGH</small> the river neighborhood. Nothing changed. The lawns were still meticulous. The outside of his mother's house overflowed with beautiful flowers and plants that Blair planted for her.

Timmy's swing set gave way to a tree fort the boys built, which then collapsed in a monster winter storm.

Nothing ever lasts — Timmy hung his head when they took it down.

Everything felt so empty now. Timmy was away at college. He was becoming a sound, audio and lights techie guy. Duncan? Not into that stuff. He was happy to lead a quiet life, helping his mother over the years.

High school was full of sports and activities. Timmy and Duncan were on the same teams, competed fiercely and wanted to go to the same university. Sadly, Duncan's grades were not quite good enough, so when Timmy got a scholarship to a fantastic school, he couldn't refuse. Duncan understood, but was sad that the two of them would be so far apart.

"Don't worry, Dunc! When I come back, we will do some cool stuff together, I promise. I'd never forget you," Timmy said as he drove away that late summer day.

McKenna looked on with Blair as Duncan waved goodbye. As he wandered away, both mothers sensed his pain. McKenna confided in Blair that the money that Ethan had been sending them over the years wasn't enough, and Financial Aid wouldn't consider them with only McKenna's part-time job at the Garden Center Blair had recently opened.

The outward appearance was still the same. The neighborhood was postcard-worthy, but the people in it had scars you couldn't see from the perfectly landscaped streets.

B lair lost Donald the year before to cancer. The man who gave her everything made sure that after he passed, she would have everything she needed to make her life worth living. She opened the Garden Center with the money he set aside for her. She named a section after him, *Donald's Daffodils.*

McKenna was her first customer.

McKenna was her first employee. Only part-time, but

it helped her get out of the house, and both of them were where they loved to be: in the open amongst the greenery, flora and the people.

They provided flowers and plants to the people who settled in James Bend; the name given to the subdivision a couple of years earlier. There were some new areas and additional abodes, still in the quaint and idyllic architecture that made the original neighborhood stick out. When Better Homes and Gardens finally featured it as an 'All-American Community', everyone wanted to live there.

There was a neighborhood pool, a few tennis courts scattered about, plus the Nursery / Pre-School near the center of it all.

Down the bank was the most beautiful and peaceful cemetery with lush green lawns and trees with full canopies of leaves, watching over those who were laid to rest within. Benches sat along the soft caress of the water as it flowed by. You couldn't help but feel at peace when you were there.

They named it *Anderson's Acre* in honor of the man who started it all with his bare hands and a vision of the life he wanted to provide for his Blair.

Blair made sure she could always see his monument, in the distance, from the window of her kitchen. The boys made sure nothing ever got overgrown or blocked her view.

Timmy has grown up a lot in the past year. Blair wanted him to stay young forever.

Now that he was away, it was just McKenna and Duncan left.

Before Timmy left for college, Duncan told him, as they were sitting by the river's edge, "Don't worry, I'll be here for her."

Timmy answered back, "I know you will. You take care of everybody."

T hose words rang through Duncan's mind as he wandered the streets.

Tennis balls resonated being hit around, and the participants arguing whether it was in or out echoed loudly in the neighborhood. He laughed to himself. He and his best friend had those same arguments.

Off in the distance, clanging horseshoes made him smile. The smell of hot dogs and burgers was in the air. Late summer never changes. The playground was a block away, but you could hear the bustle of the swings and a see-saw that needed a healthy dose of oil.

As he got closer, he noticed a bunch of kids on the

playground. One was a little closer, working on his bike. It was upside down, and the chain had popped off.

"Hey, Duncan," Reggie said. He was about 14, with a brown mop top, wearing skater shorts and a dark printed T-shirt.

"Hey, Reg, I'll give you a hand." Duncan stepped in to help. Reggie let him. In no time, it was back on, and the quick-release wheels were realigned to tighten the chain. They flipped the bike over, and Reggie was on his way with a quick wave back.

A shriek pierced the air. Duncan's head spun towards the playground next to the daycare.

A few kids were gathered in a circle around someone on the ground. She was gripping her leg. Another was holding their light jacket against it. Duncan sprinted over. Everyone there knew him, so they stepped out of the way.

"I fell..." Jamie was trying to catch her breath in between sobs. "...fell off the seesaw, and then... it came down on my leg hard. It hurts so much!" Jamie was starting to cry and panic. The others were getting worked up as well.

He peeled back the jacket. His stomach turned. The skin was torn open, and the bone was at an angle that left no doubt—broken. Blood flowed from the wound. Duncan surveyed his surroundings. He couldn't carry her all the way up the block, and the nearest house felt like it was a mile away.

Jamie was crying loudly, and the other kids were frozen in fear. Duncan felt Jamie's cries, her pain, her fear. *Inside, something pulled at him.* It was as if something took over talking for him.

"It'll be ok," he insisted, trying to calm everyone. "Turn away and don't peek."

The group did as he asked, but they were still paralyzed to run for help.

Duncan took Jamie's chin in his hand and told her, "Don't be afraid. Look right at me. It will be alright." *The pull got stronger, guiding his hands.*

He peeled the jacket off her leg, stared deep in her eyes, and covered the wound with his hand. Everything got bright around them, even on a summer afternoon.

"Jamie Marshall, Get OFF the ground and stop crying. You're fine."

The light left as quickly as it came. Jamie was standing in the middle of the group. They all turned and gawked. The only evidence of anything was the red-stained jacket and traces of blood on her leg.

Duncan was still crouched over. He was waiting a moment to collect himself.

He started to stand up, but he faltered. The group helped him.

He surveyed everyone, and their eyes were wide from what they saw.

"Nah, it wasn't so bad... just a scratch." He tried to play it off. No one would actually remember everything, so he was giving them an alternative timeline.

The kids will grasp onto that.

"Jamie, let's go up to my house, and my Mum will help clean that up before you go home," Duncan said. He acted as if nothing had happened. He took her by the hand and away they walked, towards the Drummond house.

His legs felt like rubber. *Because I squatted a long time*, he convinced himself. He didn't want to face the truth of the gift.

The group gawked at them as they moved away. They milled around, then wandered away.

Duncan and Jamie reached the house. His mother was sitting outside. A quick look at the two of them, she realized she needed to get a wet cloth. Once back outside with the damp cloth, Jamie sat on the steps, and

McKenna soothed her with her voice.

"**T**here, there, lass. A wee bit of a scrape, but t'is fine now."

McKenna cleaned her shin with care.

"Hold this for one second while I find another." She scooped up a couple of washcloths from the ground and strode into the house. Duncan smiled at Jamie, then followed his mother in.

"Mum. MUM. It happened AGAIN. Her leg was broken. She had a gash. It was bleeding. I just ...just told her it would be alright... and..." Duncan was searching for words.

She strode up to him, pressed her index finger to his lips, for him to be quiet.

He stopped talking.

They locked eyes. No words passed between them. There was no need.

They both walked back out. *She sure seems calm. Not what I expected.* Duncan watched her inspect her leg.

He smiled weakly, then brushed her cheek.

McKenna knelt next to the girl. She wiped away the little bit of dirt and blood and grinned at Jamie. She gave her a hug, put her arms on her shoulders, and said, "See, child? T'weren't so bad. Don't give it another thought. Everything is alright, innit?"

Jamie smiled back and nodded. With another smile, she dashed off down the street, back to her house.

McKenna had the blood-stained jacket behind her back.

We'll keep this under wraps for now.

Chapter Seven

THE PLAYGROUND INCIDENT, months ago, faded, but never fully went away.

Jamie came by one afternoon to thank Miss Drummond for being so kind to her that day. She confessed that the whole accident was a blur to her, but McKenna chose her words with caution in recalling the occasion.

"T'was quite a scare. I'm glad Duncan was nearby, child. He was able to help and calm everyone down. He was so worried about you, so he brought you here."

Jamie's face lit up at the mention of Duncan. "If I had an older brother, I'd want him to be like Duncan!" Jamie exclaimed.

"He's a good boy, to be sure." McKenna paused, pondered, then continued. "In any event, we got you cleaned up a wee bit and sent you on your way." As they were talking, Duncan drove up from work, got out of the car and made a beeline to where they were sitting.

"Heeeey!" Duncan called to them. Jamie bounced up and hugged him. McKenna beamed with pride at how everyone loved him. He had a new confidence in his step following the playground accident.

"How's my little blonde tornado today? You ok?" he asked. It had been almost a year since the accident. Jamie replied, looking down at her shin, "It's fine! It's like nothing ever happened." Jamie, however, had quizzical lines on her face.

"What?" Duncan asked.

She shrugged her shoulders at him. "Reggie asked me about that day. He was on his bike, pretty far away, but he could see everyone around and cloth with a lot of blood on it. If that's what he saw, wouldn't I have a scar or something?" She was uncertain, questioning what happened.

Duncan knelt down on one knee and caught her eye, "Sometimes we remember stuff way differently than they actually turned out. Things look different when we are far away," he said with confidence.

He put his hand on her shoulder and finished, "The important thing is we sorted it all out and you were okay."

Duncan had put the stained jacket in the garbage and made certain it was well hidden from view. He made sure the garbage collectors came by and took the trash that week. He wanted to be positive there wasn't anything around that related to that event.

"Yeah, he must not be remembering it right." Jamie said, shrugging her shoulders.

McKenna had been holding her breath, but she let out a sigh of relief. Duncan was in full control. She cast a knowing glance towards her son, who eyed her back, nodding.

A couple of weeks later, at one of the coffee hour socials, the women were all sitting about, bantering back and forth. It was a lazy afternoon, and the ladies liked to gather on Saturdays in the Child Care Center.

They'd talk about new furniture or their favorite cookbooks. They used to kvetch about husbands, but that stopped after Donald died.

No one wanted to bring Blair down. They all loved when she came, adored her stories and her recipes. When she talked about Donald, they let her reminisce freely.

Almost on cue, the subject would change, and they'd be off in another direction.

On this particular Saturday, Reggie's mother was

there, along with Jamie's mother. One of the other women was asking about getting a stubborn stain out of something when the first mother quipped, "Did you have to throw out Jamie's jacket? The one she was wearing the day of her accident? Reggie told me it was really stained."

Mrs. Marshall answered, looking up from her mug, "We never found it. It disappeared, so we got her a new one." She took a sip of her coffee and concluded, "Kids, always losing their things."

The redheads held their breath and exchanged glances.

McKenna confided a lot to Blair over the years since that night with Timmy. Blair didn't know all the details, but the playground accident? She picked up that Duncan had involvement. She was a wise woman, and she put 2 and 2 together—first her boy, now something with Jamie.

Blair's protection instinct kicked in and blurted out, "Lucky Duncan was there to help is wut I'm sayin. Lucky indeed, innit?"

McKenna picked up what Blair did, and pivoted the group to their favorite desserts, which ALWAYS sparked a lively discussion. The Great Dessert Debate of James Bend was always full of challenges, laughs and a few jealous side-eyes.

Today was no different.

As the arguments over fondant vs frosting raged on, McKenna moved her hand to Blair's. Nobody picked up when she reached out her pinky and gripped Blair's. She squeezed back.

An unspoken and straightforward act of gratitude.

After two hours of throwing cupcake-laced recipe bombs and firing mortars of cookie-dough projectiles, the women, sugar-shell shocked, went on their merry way. They had their marching orders to be carried out in scattered kitchens 'On The Bend'.

B lair and McKenna walked back up the street in silence towards their houses. It wasn't uncomfortable, but it was tense. Blair glanced over. McKenna's head was down, lost in thought. "Is it something you've always known about?" she inquired, breaking the silence.

"Aye." She turned to face her and stopped. "It's something I can't explain or un'nrstand. I dn'nt try to."

"All I know is it is something he 'as. I think it is something that is some'ow passed on in certain people in the Graham clan." McKenna needed to make sense of it, and telling Blair might help her understand it.

"In my clan, there is a story of a person who healed a child. I found out, years later, that man was indeed a Graham."

"My own Ethan had some sort of ability of his own, of influence and calmness. I've 'eard tales, or maybe I've dreamed them, but m'thinks Ethan is descended of this lore."

McKenna was purging.

They halted. Blair took both of McKenna's hands in hers and stood fast. She would listen all night if she had to.

"And my Duncan, when he was little, spoke of the man mentioned in our lore, Dugald. How could he know that? I've never spoken of the tales of the Highlands."

She paused, studied the sky for a moment, then continued, "He said, 'Everyone dreams about Dugald...'"

"I tried to explain it all to him, but he was younger. I'm n'sure if he was listening."

She examined Blair's soft, freckled face. She was so curious and she listened with interest.

"Duncan said to me, 'I understand Mumma.'"

"And now I accept it. Duncan has been bestowed the grace. I know not how it is used or how it is received, but the lad is a walking, living testament, and I couldn't be more blessed."

Blair pulled McKenna towards her, wrapped her arms around her and held her for a moment. They weren't crying, but a great weight had been lifted off them.

Blair took McKenna's face in her hands, pressed her forehead to hers, as they had done many times.

"Lass, He is a gift to all of us." Blair's benediction fell like a prayer on McKenna's ears.

The next morning, both women were at the Garden Center bright and early.

The mood was light, and neither spoke of the conversation from the day before. They set about their tasks of unloading the deliveries and placing stock. There was always something to water, inventory to move and certainly no shortage of customers.

Duncan was there helping unload a big delivery of evergreens and placing them in the right areas around the greenhouses. The women checked the cards attached to each bush and then directed him where to put them.

They were busy that morning. Everyone was stocking their supplies for a weekend of planting.

You can predict the weather by the crowds; Blair knew her customers.

If there is a crowd, no rain. Not for a couple of days, at least.

Early mornings were usually slow, but not today.

A few people meandered around the overflowing tables full of flowering flats. The aisles were full of casual lookers and serious botanists both.

Off on the other side, two women aimlessly looked over shorter houseplants and small ferns. The younger of the two stared off, lost in her own world of thought. To her, this was just another task to be finished.

Duncan, half finished unloading a pallet, spotted one of them pushing a cart.

"Looking for larger evergreens," she said. As she stepped forward, he caught sight of the younger woman with her—arms crossed, eyes elsewhere.

Duncan pointed deeper into the greenhouse.

"Over there, there are some that are only 2 feet. At the edge of that door leading outside, there are some that are 4 feet. Beyond that door are ones that are over 6 feet or taller."

Duncan pivoted and addressed both women together. "What are you trying to do?" he inquired.

The mother remained silent. The daughter stared into the distance and half answered the question, "She has some idea about some stuff in front of the house. Ask her."

He ignored the uninterested answer and addressed the mother. "Go over by the 4-foot bushes and I'll be there in a minute to give you a hand," he told her, and off the two of them went.

Duncan's eyes followed them for a minute, then finished unloading the pallet.

He dusted off his hands and gave them a quick rinse under the nearby hose. He dried them on his jeans and went looking for the women. They stood over by the indoor plants, so he headed to them to check if there was anything he could assist with.

As he approached, the daughter was running her fingers along a wide, broad leaf.

"Some people call those Elephant Ear, but it is really an Alocasia. It's a perennial, so it is around for more than one season."

"There are all different varieties, but they are durable, don't need constant care, and they add a lot of green in a small space. My mom loves these."

Duncan tried a more casual approach. "I thought you were finding outdoor shrubs?" Duncan prodded her outer shell. "You looking for indoor stuff too?"

"This plant caught my eye, and I just liked it. It's like a long green heart," the daughter said.

At that moment, several plants tipped over to their right. The mother was holding one with one hand, and a large display next to her teetered precariously.

"Don't move!" Duncan yelled. He sprinted to the mother, snatched the plant out of her hand and tossed it to the floor, and gently moved her aside. He grabbed the shelf and steadied it.

"See?" he pointed. "One of the supports got loose. I'll fix it." Duncan said. He made quick work of the display and turned to the mother, who was staring at the plant Duncan dropped to the ground.

"Are you alright? You're not hurt, are you?" The mother didn't lift her head.

"My late husband gave me something like that a long time ago. I had never seen another one until now. I just wanted to see it closer, so I took it off the display and I.. I guess... I bumped it."

"He... He gave it to me and, then... everything..." She couldn't continue. She started sobbing.

Duncan knelt and scooped up the plant delicately. He put the dirt back in, making sure nothing was broken. He got up in front of her and placed it in her hands.

"It's okay. As a matter of fact, I'll give that to you. That shouldn't have tipped like that. You take that for the scare that display caused you." Duncan was a shrewd businessman.

The mother looked at him, turned away and began weeping again at his kindness. *He would never grasp... my past, my mistakes... my guilt...*

Duncan's hands were drawn to grasp her shoulders. He placed them softly and paused a moment. The light bulb above him seemed to flicker, and then he spoke.

"Go on now, you're okay. I understand."

The mother spun towards him. She couldn't comprehend why she was crying. It stopped out of nowhere. She glanced down at the plant, then back at Duncan.

Years of burden disappeared in an instant.

How... how... could he understand? A jumble of thoughts ran through her head. She inspected the plant again. A tag on it drew her attention.

Hoya Love Plant - Leave in small container, prefers to be root bound.

She turned back to Duncan, who was smiling at her. He took his hands off her shoulders.

She put the plant into the cart. She side-stepped, glancing back as he walked away.

"Come on, Sarah."

Sarah, who watched this entire scene, brought the Elephant Ear plant over. She placed it in the cart, but she couldn't take her eyes off Duncan. She witnessed her mother somehow change right in front of her eyes—*but nothing changed.* She couldn't pinpoint anything.

"Sarah?" Duncan liked the name. He gazed at the plant she was holding. "Yeah... I see it. Looks like a green heart. Probably not as big as yours, though."

Sarah felt goosebumps.

Not for years! She had been numb since her father's death ...*and I'm feeling them now???*

She and her mother headed out of the greenhouse. They didn't catch Duncan steadying himself against one of the support columns after they walked away.

Duncan leaned there for a moment. He pulled himself together and bolted right to the front, hoping he'd catch up to them. He wanted to be sure she got the gift he gave her for free.

He caught up and saw they had loaded the cart with a bunch of evergreens. The plant Sarah picked was there, too. The mother was still clutching the Hoya that Duncan had given her.

They were walking towards the checkout, so he stepped between them and took over pushing. They reached the register in short order.

"We had a little accident back in the greenhouse, so I gave her this plant," Duncan told the cashier. The checkout girl smiled at Duncan and squealed, "Sure, Dunc." Sarah bristled immediately.

Was that a tinge of jealousy? HEY! He was being nice to ME!

Sarah had never been jealous, ever. She stepped closer to be directly in Duncan's line of sight.

And I don't even know this guy.

But he IS handsome, and he was so kind to my mother...

"...and the rest on the cart, give them my discount." Duncan pointed at all the plants on the cart. He looked at everything there.

"You know, that's a lot of work for you. These are too big for...—can I at least offer to take them to your car? Maybe help you plant them? Too much for just the two of you, for sure."

And I'd get to see Sarah again, but he didn't say that out loud.

"I mean, if it's alright with her." Duncan peeked at Sarah.

She sheepishly averted her eyes. She stared at the items at the register and found herself blushing, but smiling. She tucked some hair behind her ear, bit her lower lip and glanced up at Duncan, if only for a minute. The goosebumps came back so fast she got dizzy.

"Um, ah, sure," Sarah said with a schoolgirl charm.

I'm over 20 and acting like a 12-year-old with a crush!

She cast her gaze to the ground and back to Duncan.

At the next register, Blair and McKenna tried to be nonchalant, but both were giddy for Duncan. He wasn't playing catch and release.

No, he was keeping that one.

———◆O◆———

Chapter Eight

THREE MONTHS. THREE MONTHS!

Sarah was having trouble finding things for Duncan to do.

Of course, it was for her mother. *Why would he think anything else* — she pondered.

He's not stupid.

He treats her like gold.

She adores him.

Everyone does.

I do too. — It hit her like a ton of bricks as she stared into the mirror.

I mean, my mother? She had been closed off for years. She was so young, betrayed by someone she trusted!

Don't make the same mistake, Sarah. — It was her

mother's voice.

Don't assume. Don't be vulnerable.

Don't. Do. Don't. Do.

But he's so charming. He's so gentle. And he is as steady as a rock.

The goosebumps washed over her. It didn't make any sense to her.

Damn him! Why???
Fine. I don't even care. I love him. There, I said it. She waved it off.
But... I do— Her hand went from dismissive to covering her mouth in shock.

Her mother had been broaching subjects ever since their visit to the Garden Center. And her mother had NEVER talked about these things with her. She talked about being a younger mother. She confessed to the mistakes she made.

Sarah's Dad was a pillar-of-the-county kind of person. The Preacher was the other pillar.

And Sarah's mom? An impressionable woman, caught in the crosshairs. Loved by one man and seduced by the trust of another.

It destroyed her Father. He lost all purpose and direction. He meandered, rudderless without his family. One day, he wandered into Flannigan Field to hunt.

He never came out.

The affair was found out, and the preacher was excommunicated, never to be seen again.

It left Sarah and her mother alone and broken. She had been closed off for so long, and then Duncan came along and lifted the veil.

She lit up when Duncan came over. Sure, Sarah 'might have' loosened the water faucet outside. That railing? *No idea how it broke.* The small stone wall? *Must've tumbled during the last storm.*

I think he is suspicious.

"You know, you don't have to keep fooling with things so you have a reason for me to come over," Duncan said, snapping her out of her daydream.

"You .. you.. I..." Sarah stammered.
Use your words — Sarah screamed to herself.
"When... did you know?"

"That rock wall? You had me build that." Duncan started. "Days later, part of it fell, you know, like you said, because of the storm." Sarah nodded affirmatively.

"Yeah... right in the middle of that two-week heatwave—no rain, water restrictions, totally bone-dry."

Damn him! I am so busted! Sarah couldn't help but giggle inside.
Was I that transparent? Play dumb. Deny everything.

"So I went along with it. I wanted to see what you came up with."

"And Carla, your mom? She ratted you out. She's told me more than once that you've been a little disjointed lately, and I think it's all adorable. I wanna quit pretending I have to come over to fix something. I wanna come over because I want to be with you."

Damn HIM! Not only did he knock down my walls, he pulverized my defenses and built a walkway with it.— Sarah surrendered.

She didn't have to pretend anymore.

Other than work, they were almost as inseparable as Duncan and Timmy had been years ago. Blair had a brief twinge seeing them so close, but when Timmy came home from college with a new lady, Veronica, in his life, she was able to breathe easy.

The couples did things together. They did stuff apart. McKenna, Blair and Carla were a shopping force. Everyone could be interchanged at a second's notice—a large extended family. Holidays were special. Fireplace-toasted marshmallows and cocoa nights were warm, cozy, and as low-key as you could ask for.

One night, they were all huddled around the hearth in Blair's house. Sarah took note—*of course it was perfect. Blair means 'Perfect' in Scottish, right?*

Duncan spoke first as everyone relaxed and enjoyed the quiet. "I have to work all this week, but I have some time off in February. Maybe the four of us could go skiing." Duncan's idea floated over the group.

"I'd be terrified. I've never tried," Sarah confessed.

Timmy, who might have had a little nip (or three) in his cocoa, blurted out, "Don't worry, Dunc will take care of you!" He was a lot louder than he usually was. Under the blanket, Blair poked Timothy in the ribs with her toe.

"What, Ronnie knows all about it!" Timmy got another kick.

"Well, it's getting late, and I have to head home. Early day in the office for me tomorrow!" Carla chimed in, unaware of the conversation pothole they narrowly missed.

They all got up and stretched. Blair grabbed hold of Timmy's ear and twisted. Timmy's memory kicked in, and he quieted right down.

As Carla headed out the door, she asked Duncan to drive Sarah home later, when the plows had a chance to clean the streets. Duncan suggested she should wait too, but she stubbornly wanted to get to bed with such an early day coming up.

The door closed behind her. They waved as she crept along, driving down the snow-laden street. She turned the corner two blocks down.

Two hours went by. Duncan dropped Sarah off at her house and walked her to the door. They were laughing as they fell into the front room. They didn't think anything of the lights not being on. The street lamps cast an eerie glow through the living room window.

Sarah moved through the door to turn on the lamp. As she reached for the lamp, she glanced at the red light flashing on the answering machine. She pressed play as she clicked on the light.

BEEP
Duncan earlier in the day.
BEEP
McKenna was saying something, but her accent garbled it.

Sarah cast a coy look towards Duncan. She worshipped him almost as much as he adored her. She couldn't believe how...

BEEP

"Is this the Griffin Residence? This is James River Medical Center. There has been an accident, and you need to contact us as soon as you receive this. James River police are en route to your house to provide transportation."

CLICK

Duncan and Sarah gazed at each other, expressionless. She turned and looked back at the answering machine, hoping there was another message.

There wasn't.

It has to be a mistake.

As they tried to comprehend what they had just listened to, the police lights filled the room from the streets.

E verything was a blur. The police took the two of them on the 10-minute ride to the Medical Center. The radio crackled with action, but you couldn't understand it.

Why did I let her go alone? Duncan beat himself up. *Get me to the hospital. I don't care who finds out now. Sarah will find out, but I don't care.*
I DON'T CARE.

The squad car pulled up to the emergency room entrance. The police opened the doors, and Duncan dragged Sarah in with him.

I don't care WHO finds out!

Staff waited inside the door. A nurse and two doctors confronted them. They spoke to Sarah like no one else was there.

"Sarah Griffin? I am Dr. McGinty, and this is Dr. Bales, a couple of the Residents here in the ER. Your mother was in an accident with a drunk driver. That driver crossed the median at a high rate of speed..."

"Let me see her." Sarah implored, frightened and wide-eyed.

They continued, "...it was over in an instant. She didn't suffer." They paused at the words they had probably said too many times in their careers. "We regret to inform you that your Mother did not survive."

Sarah's tortured scream rang through the emergency room corridors. She collapsed on the cold tile floor, sobbing.

Why did I let her LEAVE????? — Duncan broke down. He was so close to stopping her, but didn't.

He moved towards Sarah and tried to lift her off the floor, but she wouldn't let him touch her.

Not then.

For the rest of the week, Sarah couldn't bring herself to move. She lay in an empty house that was shattered beyond anything she imagined.

She hadn't finished her conversation with her Mother! She didn't hear the complete story! Why or how it all happened, that explanation was wiped from the face of the earth.

I didn't even tell her I forgave her — Weeping would pounce on her at random moments.

Blair and McKenna took turns staying with her, making sure she ate. They wouldn't allow her to deal with any of the arrangements. Everyone from that night felt guilty and wanted to do what they could to help her.

As alone as she was, people surrounded her, not just propping her up. They let her wilt, get emotional, stand, stumble and regain her legs.

She found strength through the will of others.

Even from Duncan.

McKenna and Blair brought his crude hand drawings over. She would open them, smile and then the tears would come.

I can't ever suffer this pain again. I can't... — Sarah would not let Duncan that close. If he weren't any closer, then she'd never have to face pain like this ever again.

The day of the wake came. There was still so much to take care of, and Sarah had no idea what needed to be done. Her fog was lifting, but there was no defined way forward. No direction. No purp...

Blair came to her side, clad in a black dress adorned with the whitest pearls Sarah had ever seen. Sarah stared in the mirror and realized she was wearing the same dress.

How did... Is this real?

Blair saw the fog in Sarah's eyes. She turned her away from the mirror.

"Face me, child." Blair urged her.

She took off the pearls and placed them around Sarah's neck. She turned her back towards the hallway mirror. Sarah didn't recognize the reflection staring back at them.

Blair leaned in and whispered to Sarah, "I wore these when I laid my Donald down, may he Rest In Peace. You wear them today for your Mother." She felt Blair's hands on her shoulders.

"Dun'na worry, child, everything has been arranged. Your mother will watch over us, a few scant feet from my Donald." Sarah ran her hands along the necklace. Blair looked on, acting as her guide.

"It's time to go. Now it's time to be the Lady of the House. Hide your grief and taake a brave face out of the closet and put it on."

"Your grief is only suitable for one thing. And you dun'na need it anymore."

Sarah closed her eyes tightly one last time. A long, heavy breath passed over her lips. She glanced up and looked in the mirror. One last moment of silence gently parted like a curtain.

Sarah turned and kissed Blair on the cheek. She pulled her shoulders back. Her eyes were clear. The brave face had made its appearance.

"I'm ready." Sarah opened the front door. The women headed to the limo waiting for them.

The car door was open. McKenna, Timmy and Veronica were inside.

Sarah climbed in, followed by Blair. Once they settled in, McKenna leaned forward and said, "Duncan wanted to be here, but he made sure I gave this to you." She took the bag and opened it.

It contained a small Elephant Ear plant.

I can't believe he... The brave face had a small crack in it. There were plenty of tissues for *everyone* on the ride.

Within the Chapel, outside the neighborhood, there were dozens of people waiting. All of them were from James Bend. Sarah didn't think they knew who she was, but they were all there for her. They appreciated that this was Duncan's woman.

Blair and McKenna didn't have to lift a finger to rally the community this time.

They made their way to the Altar and sat in the front pews. Blair, Timmy and Veronica, on the right side, facing the simple casket. Sarah and McKenna, on the left. Sarah was staring straight ahead, looking at all the flowers. She glanced to her left and noticed that McKenna had put some space between them.

Maybe she wants to give me... — a blurred figure passed by and stopped in front of the casket. They placed two potted plants in front, where they could be seen by all.

Hoya Love Plants

Duncan stood up, turned and took his place next to Sarah.

The rest of the service faded in her ears.

In the receiving line, she couldn't make out what people were saying to her. It was just a blur. Even when Duncan came through, she was still in a mist she couldn't quite pierce.

The next thing she knew, she was sitting by herself in the front pew.

McKenna, Blair and the others sat in pews behind her, at a respectful distance.

Sarah stared straight ahead and surveyed the simple yet beautiful casket. In her distant memory, she heard Blair's voice.

Fancy is for us; simple is everything she needs.

Sarah received so many hugs, so many hands of comfort, so many people stroking her hair in sorrow; another was inevitable. But when the hand on the back of her head moved to stroke her cheek, she closed her eyes. She felt the goosebumps. She realized Duncan was there.

Duncan directed her face forward, towards the casket. His hands moved to her shoulders. His grip was soft, but it was reassuring. Warmth washed over her, and the room filled with light.

It was as if the heavens opened a door and guided Carla home.

The ethereal glow faded.

Sarah's fog lifted. She couldn't feel the sorrow she had felt for the past week. She had the memory, but not the anguish.

Duncan struggled to seat himself behind her. Once he did, he bowed his head. He didn't let on that sitting was the only thing he could do, for the moment.

Blair came forward after a few moments and gathered everyone together.

The group filed out in silence, got in the limo and trailed the hearse to Anderson's Acre.

The crowd at the church was all present. They parted as Sarah and the others approached.

Sarah walked ahead of everyone else. Alone.

The rest of the group followed behind.

The Lady of the House.

Blair coached her well. No words were said, no prayers were offered. The silence covered the wounds with delicate care.

If you squinted, you could see it, but it started slow. McKenna grabbed Blair's pinky with her own. Blair grabbed Timothy's. Timothy grabbed Veronica.

Soon, everyone in the Acre stood bound by something beyond themselves.

Duncan turned to everyone, then to Sarah.

Chin held high, Sarah reached for Duncan's pinky. He took it on one side, and McKenna's on the other.

A chain forged in flesh, bound by love, strengthened by silence.

Blair turned first. She kissed Sarah's forehead and moved towards the gate. She stopped for a moment, kissed her fingertips, then pressed them to Donald's marker. Others followed suit until the only ones left were Duncan and Sarah.

She faced Duncan and made one last request.

"Drive me home."

They pulled up to the Griffin house. McKenna, Blair, Veronica and Timmy were waiting.

T wo months later, the Gingers...

They love being called that— Sarah chuckled, but they embraced it.

...pulled together a Celebration of Life at the Day Care Center which had been repurposed for a day, as a rec center.

Everyone came out—tables in the yard, lots of food brought in by all the participants. A TV played a video of different scenes from Carla's life. Sarah included pictures of her father and the three of them as a family.

She was trying to find peace, and this was her path there, when suddenly, a motorcycle raced by, breaking the peace for a moment. Everyone stopped to see who it was, but no one saw the rider.

Today of all days! Sarah eventually looked back at all the people gathered for her mother.

Laughter filled the air, and people wandered around and stopped, just to talk—kids, adults, teenagers and a few old folks, all scattered about. It was a large family reunion for the neighborhood.

Duncan stood outside the fenced-in area, ready to grab any balls that came over the fence, into the street.

"Dunc!" a voice cried out.

Duncan spun around and saw Jamie Marshall standing there. Away for a couple of years, and here she was back from her Sophomore year at college, Nursing School. Duncan had a special place in his heart for his adopted little sister.

"Oh, my! Look at you!"

'Old Man' Graham grabbed a nearby bat, used it like a cane and hobbled towards Jamie. "I feel REALLY old right now. Not fair. Not fair at all." They embraced like family.

Sarah poked fun at them. "Trading me in for a newer model already?"

Jamie teased back, "He's all mine. Mine, mine, MINE!" Everyone laughed.

Everyone adores him, but that's MY man. Sarah's smile lit up her face.

A voice cracked the air like a whip.

"HEY DUNCAN." You couldn't quite locate where it came from. Heads turned to find the source.

"HEY DUNCAN!" This time, the voice was closer. A tall, lanky teenager called from his motorcycle, parked between two cars.

"HEY, REMEMBER ME? REGGIE? I KNEW YOU'D BE HERE."

He took a deep swig from his bottle. It wasn't water, to be sure.

Timmy hopped the fence and got between Reggie and Duncan.

"Don't bother..." Reggie knocked Timmy to the ground. Everyone slowed down and stopped.

Reggie had a long history of trouble, and no one wanted to set him off. People backed up. The gate to the fenced area opened with caution.

Duncan, with no fear, walked towards Reggie, his soothing voice trying to keep everyone calm. He casually tossed the bat to the side, sticking out his right hand.

"Hey Reg. Let's go for a walk and catch up. It sure has been a long time."

"CUT THE CRAP. YOU'RE SO FAKE. AND NO ONE BELIEVED ME. THEY ALL BELIEVED YOU. NOT ME. I WAS THE ONE THEY WHISPERED ABOUT WHEN THEY SHOULD BE TALKING ABOUT YOU."

Reggie gazed around at the crowd to be sure people were hearing him.

He pulled a knife from the sheath on his belt. "NO ONE BELIEVED ME. NO ONE! THEY TALKED ABOUT ME LIKE I HAVE A PROBLEM."

McKenna, without thinking, stepped forward. Duncan put his hand up to keep her in her place.

"LET'S SHOW EM WHAT YOU CAN DO"

Reggie drew the blade across his finger, and the blood appeared on cue.

"GO AHEAD, FIX THAT"

A shriek rang out, and the crowd scattered in different directions.

"GO AHEAD, SHOW THEM. FIX IT!!!"

"Reggie, I can't..." Duncan was still talking when Timmy jumped on top of Reggie and wrestled him to the ground.

Panic was in full effect. People were running in every direction. Yells echoed from all sides. People were squeezing through the gate to move away. Duncan stepped towards where Timmy and Reggie were on the ground.

Tires screeched. A scream shot through everyone like a knife.

Duncan's head whipped around. All he could see were feet on the ground.

He ran to the spot.

JAMIE

She had been hit by a car and was unconscious on the road. Her leg was twisted impossibly under her. Blood was staining the road.

"No, no, no no NO!" *This is my fault,* Duncan cursed under his breath. Not her. Not now. He was pulled towards Jamie. His hands found her shoulders. The warmth consumed him.

"Jamie Marshall, Get OFF the ground. You're fine!"

A blinding light.

A deafening silence.

Jamie stood there. She glanced around and then down at Duncan.

He was on his knees. Realizing what had happened, he started to sob.

Now everyone knows.

————————◆○◆————————

Chapter Nine

THE WORLD GOT a lot smaller after that. It got a lot faster, too.

The entire town wanted a piece, a touch, a call, a quote. It didn't stop.

McKenna tried to talk to Duncan, to prepare him. She saw it with Ethan, years ago. Lochlan accepted Ethan, and the Drummond clans folk would solicit his goodness to the point of exhaustion when he would come to the village. Most wanted his counsel and nothing more. He tended many in both villages.

She sensed Duncan would need all the support he could get. Blair's heart tore to see the boy she watched grow up be ripped in a hundred directions. Sarah had several weak moments of her own.

Duncan knew what the questions were; she didn't have to ask.

What was he?
Who is he?

What did he DO to my mother?
What did he do to ME?

She caught the whispers.

Did you see what he did?
Was Reggie right all along?

Even Jamie had her doubts. What exactly happened when she was younger? *Miss Drummond, did she know??*

Duncan sensed a difference in the way Sarah studied him. The James Bend neighborhood went from almost picture perfect to a cage overnight.

How could my world change like this? I didn't do anything wrong. I did everything with pure intentions. I saved Jamie. I tried to reach out to Reggie. I showed up for Sarah. I gave Carla's mind peace!

TIMMY!

No word from him in days.

Did he get hurt? Duncan panicked.

He bolted out of his house and sprinted over to Blair's place.

He burst through the door, breathless.

Veronica and Blair sat at the kitchen table. They

turned, and Duncan spotted Timmy sitting in front of a pile of papers and flyers.

Timmy didn't hesitate. He got up and sidestepped the mess and embraced Duncan. One hand moved to hold the back of his head. His other arm wrapped around his back. "You did nothing wrong. NOTHING," Timmy whispered. The embrace said it all.

"Are you okay?" Timmy asked. Blair reached out and grabbed his hand. Ronnie got up and helped Duncan into her vacated seat. He surveyed them, confused.

"Duncan, Timmy wants to show you something," Veronica said. She pushed Timmy to sit down. "Tell him your idea." She nudged Timmy.

"You're not evil. People don't comprehend what happened. I don't think even you know." Timmy started, reading Duncan's face.

"I wish I knew," he replied.

"Nobody does. I don't think anyone knows what, or who or how." Timmy continued.

"We need to be ahead of this. We have to lay it out. We are going to reveal to them who you are."

Duncan's eyes widened. He leaned forward.

"Give me 48 hours to put it in motion. I can help."

The two women were nodding in agreement. Duncan hesitated, then nodded in agreement as well.

"Do what you think is best." Duncan had no idea what that could be.

Timmy got busy. He disappeared while he hustled. He made calls. He was all over the neighborhood. He talked to everyone. Veronica wasn't sure if he slept.

True to his word, two days later, in the morning, Timmy showed up at McKenna's house unannounced.

"You two, come with me. Right now." Sarah and Duncan traded looks over their breakfast plates, but jumped up and followed him out the door.

"In the car. Don't ask me questions." He had a purpose now. They drove for a few minutes and pulled into a church parking lot.

"We are going inside." Timmy's madness consumed him. He opened the doors. It took a minute for everyone's eyes to adjust.

Several people were inside. Jamie was the closest. She got up and came to Duncan.

"I'm sorry. I have no reason not to believe in you." Mrs. Marshall echoed her daughter, "I can never thank you enough. I realize that now."

Blair stood up next. "Don't ever doubt yourself. I don't."

McKenna stepped forward. "We all accept you. And we will all protect you."

Duncan scanned everyone present. A hand touched his forearm. Sarah locked eyes with him. She drew a deep breath.

"I don't know what it is, but I've always trusted you. I have confidence in you now. Tell us what we need to do." She glanced over her shoulder at Timmy.

"Everyone, do what I asked them to do and come back tomorrow," Timmy told them. They all nodded and went their separate ways.

The following morning, McKenna drove Duncan and Sarah back to the church. They turned down the street that it was on. Parked cars littered the road. The parking lot? Packed.

One empty spot at the side door, and McKenna took it. The space was marked 'RESERVED'.

As Duncan climbed out of the back seat, McKenna blocked him at the car door. The sunlight played off her fiery red hair, and her eyes stared into Duncan's core.

"Yer Faather told me once he was 'pulled' to do the things that he did. Now I witness my own boy answer the very same calling."

"Stand as a Graham. Courage and strength will come to youu. Guide you, it will, that." She reached out, eyes welling with pride, and took his right hand.

She brought it to her lips and whispered, "Go with the Grahams who have come before youu. Their strength is yours to carry forward."

She stepped aside, keeping her head bowed. Duncan gazed upon her, paused, then strode past her towards the door.

Timmy was waiting for them.

"What's all this? What are we doing?" Hard to put the puzzle together if you don't know what the pieces look like.

"Speak your heart, Duncan." Timmy pleaded. "That's never wrong."

He stepped inside and walked through the darkened hallway. He approached the closed door.

A deep breath. Another.
His hand grabbed the handle. He drew the door back.

He stepped into everyone's eyes.
Utter silence.

He peered into the darkness. It was dim inside. He couldn't focus his eyes very well.

One by one, the lights above illuminated. Each showed more and more rows of people.

Some in wheelchairs. Some on crutches. Some seated.

Not a voice could be heard.

Duncan Graham saw the small podium and ambled up to it. He fumbled to adjust the microphone. The noise echoed in the hushed hall.

"I don't want anyone to fear me. I can't ex..." he paused. His statement would carry weight.

Keep it simple, so a child would understand.

He searched the crowd's eyes. His gaze settled on Sarah. Her eyes were wide, full of hope and wonder.

Do the right thing... Sarah's message to him. Her father used to say that to her, she had told Duncan months ago.

"I can't explain it. It just happens. I can't control whatever it is. I can't just do it." Duncan spoke, hesitating.

"I wish I could, but I can't... and ... and that may disappoint some people." He scoured the room again. So many people were staring at him—*for something.*

All I know is that you should always strive to do for yourself. — Say it! Say those words! Duncan was screaming inside.

"Try to do for yourself. If you have to, turn to others for help. That's okay if you do."

"I can't do everything myself, but I have those who support me. I am sure you have people who will help you."

Duncan was finding his stride. Sarah's hands covered her mouth in shock. Where was this all coming from?

She couldn't help but be drawn to it. Apparently, so were others in the church.

"If you can't do it by yourself, ask for help. Then give help to someone else. If you can't help yourself or someone else, come here."

"Perhaps, among the rest of us, we can be the help you need."

Duncan could feel the warmth building inside him. It singed without pain, yet it still burned.

Many in the church were on their feet. It was

still silent, but everyone was fixated on Duncan. He suddenly realized the beam of light, filtering from the rafters, belonged to him alone.

Timmy hoped something like this would happen. He wanted to be sure he rigged a follow spot to track Duncan if it did. It did its job flawlessly.

It allowed Duncan's light to be seen by all.

His gaze wandered. Eyes that had been curious and fearful before were full of hope now.

You gave them the nudge; now it's time to guide them. His purpose was never clearer.

McKenna viewed her son from a distance. Their paths separated here.

His journey had just begun.

Duncan stepped off the dais. Sarah met him and embraced him, her cheeks damp with tears. She didn't even know why she was crying. He gently stroked her face. The warmth consumed him. Timmy came up behind him, put his hands on his shoulders and leaned his head on his back.

This is your calling — the words repeated in Timmy's head.

Blair reached out and touched him. So did all the

others.

Not out of desperation, but for connection. Not a single person left. They all waited to touch Duncan, or were content to let him pass by. They were all here to see him.

Duncan made sure he tended to all that came—one after another.

Hours later, the church was almost vacant. Duncan moved towards the door he had come in. He was a lot more wobbly than when he came in.

Did I... — He recognized the physical symptoms, but he didn't remember anyth—

In the corner, he spotted them.

A youngster stood there and looked at Duncan with reverence.

A father, behind him. Holding on to an empty wheelchair.

The father lowered his head, as if to acknowledge Duncan. Duncan did the same. The child stepped forward, unsteady at first. He made his way to Duncan, holding on to the rows of pews as he moved closer.

The boy stopped in front of him, his gaze fixed. Duncan dropped to one knee and got face-to-face with the child.

"You're fine now," he said.

The boy answered, "I ... I... think I am."

With that, he turned, headed back to his father, and they exited.

Sometimes, you don't even see that you were part of the miracle.

Timmy helped Duncan up and moved towards the door. Duncan needed to get home to rest.

This scene repeated itself for the next several months. It got to where they had to have two seatings a day. Soon, they outgrew the old abandoned church.

People offered ideas for a new location. Suggestions were pouring in, and 'go-see' lists were filled fast. Timmy and Duncan went and checked them all out.

One day, someone offered a ride to take them to check out potential places. After driving for a few hours and looking at different locations, they returned to Duncan's house.

The person handed Duncan the keys. "This is a donation." That's all they said. Duncan couldn't believe it. A three-row SUV? How did anyone know his car was help together with wire and duct tape?

When you look out for everyone... most of them watch out for you.

L ater that night, Duncan wanted to take his inner circle out to show his appreciation. There were so many who wished to be near Duncan, but he pined for something quiet and personal.

Blair and McKenna, Timmy and Veronica, Duncan and Sarah. They all got in Duncan's newly donated car.

They drove out of James Bend and went one town over, hoping for something uneventful.

McKenna spotted a small corner pub and begged Duncan to stop. It was quaint, oozed a friendly vibe, with plants and some outdoor seating. It was still a little light out, so the petals on the flowers and the fairy lights strung all over the shrubs were visible.

They parked out back. McKenna stuck her head inside, asking if they could sit outside and put a few tables together. The owner obliged and came out to move them himself.

They were all seated, and the owner brought some water and bread over.

Timmy spoke up, "Dunc, I really liked that last place we checked out. Let's take it. Let me spruce it up and install a few things to help with the meetings. Little extras here and there."

"Can we take everyone over to see it first?" Duncan wanted everyone's input.

"Sure, we can go by tomorrow."

No one spotted the waitress standing nearby—until Sarah looked up and blurted, "Howdy!" The backwoods in her voice had a knack for showing up at the worst times.

The waitress was tall and blonde, her long, wavy hair pulled back in a ponytail. She was breathtaking—perfect nails, flawless skin, clothes that looked tailor-made. She had full lips over a small button nose—cool blue eyes framed by long, luxurious eyelashes. There was nothing her stunning, subdued makeup had to hide.

She's gotta be a model. Sarah caught herself staring.

"My name's Hannah, and I'll be your server tonight. So glad y'all are here!" She gave the group a warm sweep with her eyes.

"Anyone want me to grab them some Iced Tea or Lemonade, or maybe something a bit more grow'd up?"

Her gaze settled right on Sarah.

"What can I git you, Shugah?"

Timmy jumped in. "Tell me about..."

Hannah cut him off at the knees. "Ewwwwee..." she laughed, giving him a poke with her pencil. "...gon' wait your turn. I was talkin' to the prettiest lady here, I do believe."

She's a lil hellfire! Veronica giggled. Timmy's ego just got stomped, so he hung his head appropriately. Veronica gave him an affectionate pat on his head to make the bruises hurt a little less.

Sarah froze. That accent—pure West Virginia, and too familiar. The one she had buried ages ago was standing right in front of her.

I have to get to know this girl. She peeked at Duncan with a mischievous smile.

Maybe she can help me find my attitude again. That would be dangerous.

The evening rambled on, like a lazy beach day, full of laughs. The owner and Hannah pulled up chairs to join the fun. Duncan received most of the jokes, but he just smiled and laughed with everyone else. He knew getting picked on was a sign of affection, so he invited it. Every time someone took a shot, Duncan would grin and stare at the ground. Sarah's gaze never left him. She marveled at how comfortable he could be in any situation. He never made a joke at anyone's expense.

Hannah noticed Sarah's constant dreamy stare at Duncan. She recognized the look. Hannah had it for someone, long ago.

The banter was warm, and everyone got involved. Duncan listened to those closest to him and welcomed everyone having their space to talk. The Pub Owner, unsuccessfully, tried to pin names on everyone sitting there. He finally gave up and asked for help.

Everyone at the table introduced themselves.

Duncan went last. He stood up, extended his hand and said, "I'm..."

Hannah jumped in, "... Lucky." She stared right at Sarah and gave her a wink.

Sarah's heart almost burst out of her chest.

"That woman will take care of you until the Good Lord calls you home." Hannah's tone was dead serious.

"I believe she will," Duncan replied. He stared right at Sarah. The goosebumps arrived. They were predictable.

The owner asked, "So tell me your name before these ladies gang up on you."

"Duncan Graham,"

"You mean..." The owner's surprise was visible.

"Just Duncan Graham, okay?"

Hours later, Timmy asked for the check, but the owner declined to give it to him. He refused to give it to anyone. He merely asked that they come back again.

Sarah said, "Oh, we will absolutely be back."

They left, tired and stuffed. And now, their little circle was a bit bigger.

How could you not love the Innkeeper or his little lass? — McKenna's old-school vibe was on display.

The following day, they all travelled to the Old Baptist Worship House, which had closed a few years before. It was in the adjoining county, but not a long drive.

Timmy showed the place off and explained how he planned to install some lighting and a state-of-the-art sound system, because, "I want everyone to hear..." It wouldn't resemble a church, but it would have its own community vibe.

"I trust in what you want to do. You know that world way better than I do. Let's make it special." Duncan charged Timmy with making it happen.

The work slipped into high gear. Demolition. Construction. Wiring. Finish chores. More than one night at the pub outside of town. Some nights, Hannah was the waitress. A few of the nights, Hannah was at the table with them, not serving them, and they all quickly became friends.

Sarah and Hannah were given a pet name. No one knows who came up with it, but it fit them perfectly.

The 'Mountain Gals' used to come by the new Hall to see the progress often.

Mountain Gals, is that what they ge t' callin' us? Hannah's electrifying smile hid her glee at the name.

And all the while, people would stop by to be near Duncan, and he always gave them the attention they deserved. He never complained. The warmth never left him. It never failed him when it counted.

Hannah had never seen anything like it. She told Sarah, more than once, how lucky she was to know them both.

Sarah noticed too.

A host of fresh faces joined the crew working on the project to complete it. People would show up to be near Duncan and what he was trying to build.

Alan was one of the new faces.

McKenna brought him to the pub one night. He had a swarthy Scottish brogue, laughed easily and fit in well with the group. He took to being a logistics standout and Timmy's right-hand man. If you needed something, Alan was the man. He kept Timmy focused on the overall project and let him lead.

Duncan found out later that Alan was McKenna's nephew from back in Scotland.

She didn't speak of it a lot, but when she did, Duncan paid attention. He was a cousin by blood and wore his Drummond Clan bloodlines on his sleeve.

He lifted McKenna's spirits when he spoke of the land she missed so dearly. They were often in the corner talking alone. Other times, Alan could be seen engaging with almost everyone. Days dragged into weeks. Weeks slogged into months.

One afternoon stuck out to Duncan.

Alan was off with McKenna in a corner, but things were not as light as usual. It was daytime, and they sat in front of a window, so all you could see were the silhouettes against the glass backdrop. Alan was talking, kneeling in front of her.

McKenna's head fell forward onto his shoulder. Her sobbing permeated the air.

Duncan started towards his mother, but Timmy caught his arm. "They need to do this alone," Timmy whispered. He hugged Duncan and led him away.

Duncan took one last look back and saw Alan take a card from his pocket and hand it to McKenna. She pressed it to her heart and crumpled on Alan's shoulder again.

Duncan never found out what transpired.

Alan had a lot of secrets that no one understood. Other times, Alan was a bundle of energy, and no one knew where it might land.

More than once, Alan would cry out, "Oy, yer jus' a Graham, whaadah u knooo? Du I hafta teach you e'rything?" A hearty belly laugh and a quick smile always followed.

S pring gave way to a Summer filled with goals and milestones, some impossible to reach. Somehow, they were always met.

One night in late August, at the pub, the inner circle gathered. It was mostly small talk, but everyone listened when Duncan spoke.

Duncan always brought attention to someone's accomplishments. A new partner charity, Blair's flower arrangements, Timmy and Veronica getting married soon. McKenna's new hairstyle, even Hannah bringing her boy by in the next week to meet the crew.

That night, however, after giving everybody a moment to shine, he paused.

They waited anxiously, but Duncan shut his eyes and let time linger.

The air was light. Late summer. Aroma of seasonal flowers in bloom. A breeze wafted through the trees.

He turned to Sarah, took her by the hand and stood her up for all to see.

As if on cue, a gentle guitar drifted to the leaves, dancing in the air.

Alan had taken it from the wall inside the pub. No one had noticed. McKenna clued him in on what was going to happen; Alan did the rest.

Duncan looked at Sarah while still holding her hand.

Duncan let the warmth build.

Sarah's goosebumps rose.

Duncan gazed into her eyes and began, unsure what to say.

"I am blessed with something I don't understand. But you help me make sense when I can't do it myself."

I never tire of this feeling. Sarah thought. Duncan made her head spin.

"I am fortunate to be able to bless others, and the joy of helping others is what we celebrate every day."

"But there is one blessing I've yet to receive."

Duncan dropped to one knee. The guitar fell silent.

"Bless me with becoming my wife."

Duncan took her left hand and placed his mother's Jeweled Claddagh ring upon her finger. Sarah knew about the treasure Ethan had given to McKenna so many years ago. Her right hand shot up to cover the gasp escaping her lips.

Stunned, she turned towards McKenna. The smile told her everything in a single glance.

Sarah stepped forward, wrapped her arms around Duncan's head and drew him close to her heart.

"May the road rise to meet us, together."

Everyone stood in bliss, watching Duncan completely surrender himself to the woman that was once trapped herself.

Leaves rustled in the gentle breeze. Birdsong floated above them. Sarah's gentle tears washed over Duncan's head, still pressed to her heart.

Alan broke the stillness; his thick Scottish brogue was so appropriate in the moment.
As fair are thou, my bonie lass,
So deep in luve am I;
And I will luve thee still, my Dear,
Till a' the seas gang dry.

To family and friends, the ties that bind us, the love that sustains us.

Alan raised his glass. Everyone followed his lead.

As McKenna looked on, her eyes welled with tears. She hadn't heard Burns since her father recited bedtime poems to her, decades ago.

"To the man I'm supposed to hate..." He paused, his gaze meeting Duncan's, the smile fading away.
"...but can't."

Chapter Ten

"**B**IRCH RIVER, WEST VIRGINIA. Small town. Big Mountains. Big boring," Hannah explained to Sarah over a couple of glasses of Pinot.

Sarah took in her finger candy. Hannah grabbed her hand and admired it herself. "Can you imagine getting his Mumma's ring?" Hannah asked.

"My Granny promised me hers when it was my time. Heeee was the one. He got it from my Mama, and I thought he was fixin' to..." Hannah paused. She took a sip of her wine. She cast her eyes to the floor, almost ashamed. "He t'were't the man I had prayed for."

"It's all about gittin' yerself somethan warm on a cold night. All it was fer him. The second he could scat, he did. And took the raang, pawned it and blew outta town."

Sarah knew her pain. "Wasn't he ever good to you? Y'all such a ray of sunshine! I am sure you had yer pick of the boys." Sarah's mountain accent was creeping back the more time she was around Hannah.

"He was baptised in dirty water, a good God fearing man. He hid everything deep, and no one caught on until it was too late." Hannah was laying her heart bare. "He lost his job, lost his Mama, lost his way. Found out I was pregnant and he couldn't figgure out how we'd make it." Hannah sighed and resigned herself to the harsh truth.

"He was an Angel at the top of the bottle, but I wasn't enough to keep him from the bottom."

Sarah knew it wasn't Hannah's fault that her man dove deeper than he should.

Sarah laid her own soul out—same spirit but different pain. "My family was from a hard place—Iron Gate. Backwoods, lots of hardship. Strings of broken families, like mine. I hated it there and what it did to us," Sarah said, walking the edge she had grasped too well.

Hannah leaned over and put her hand gently on Sarah's arm. "Baby, don't do that. 'Sall wasted." She had a way of making the hardest feeling melt away.

Sarah didn't know how to process that. No one ever cared enough to carry her weight.

"My kin wuz poor too, more ways than one. Mumma died, Daddy's heart busted, he joined her a year later. Two brothers and a sister just tryin' to survive."

"But with a broke family and a man that treated me like an old beer can, I've got my Jacob. Named him after my Daddy. He is my light and my path."

Sarah's tone softened. "I can't wait to meet him!"

How could an angel like you have a 10-year-old?

Sarah's head spun like a whirlpool.

How can you be so refreshing?
Do you know how stunning you are?

Sarah had never had a spirit like Hannah's in her life.

"You better watch out," Hannah's eyes twinkled. "Jacob might be crushin' on you, pretty lady."

If he's anything like you, Duncan has some competition — Sarah smiled to herself.

The conversation went on almost all night. By the time Sarah got home, Duncan was fast asleep on the couch.

MEN. They can fall asleep anywhere.

She curled next to him on their sectional and played her 'little spoon' part to perfection.

T he previous night forgotten, Sarah sauntered into the Hall with a couple dozen doughnuts for the team. Activity was buzzing all around. Timmy was on a walkie-talkie, directing his tech crew and making sure audio was working everywhere. Lights flashed and changed colors all over the ceiling.

A brand new Dais and staging area were moving up and down on a lift system so everyone had a better view. A fresh set of video screens had a test pattern on them, the last fine tuning so Duncan could be viewed more easily.

She marveled at what the space became in 6 short months. She stood in the middle and surveyed the entire room.

How do I describe this to someone?

She was dressed in a muted brown pantsuit, with heels, gracing her lean lines and shoulder-length, wavy light brown hair. It was pulled up in a slight bun... but still had the perfect messy look to it. Looking stylish, even in this crazy construction zone, she paused, turned a full circle, and took it all in. People had been donating and heeding Duncan's words to help each other. Duncan and Sarah witnessed the direct effect.

People reached out, and as a bonus, those same people wanted to display their appreciation to the very people who called them to action.

"Excuse me, Miss Griffin?" a boyish voice asked.

Sarah scanned a handsome and well-dressed preteen holding a flower up to her.

She grinned, looked around to see if anyone was watching, then opened one of the boxes and said, "Trade yah."

Jacob grabbed a strawberry-frosted doughnut and handed Sarah the single yellow Daffodil.

She stared as Jacob ran over to Hannah to show her the doughnut. She tilted her head toward him, and he fed her a bite. Sarah spied something wrong with his wrist, but it didn't seem to bother him.

He's gonna crush on ME? — Hannah's boy was as adorable as they come. *He's an angel's son... Of course he is...*

As Sarah started over, Alan wrapped up quickly, but she caught the end. "I'll be sure it's taken care of..."

Alan headed off, and Jacob trailed close behind with a clipboard nearly as big as he was. "Do you think he'll mind being my boyfriend if I am married?" Sarah asked when she reached Hannah. The two giggled. They slipped into silliness, like a comfy pair of slippers.

"Oh girl, you shush your sheesh!" Hannah threw a very phony surprised look at her. "Well, I never..." She paused a second and smiled.

"I've got his lil' league bat at home to hep fight off the girls." Hannah's drawl dripped with love for her boy.

She turned to face Sarah and deadpanned, "I *will* start with you, if'n it comes to thaaait..." She pointed a perfectly manicured finger at Sarah's nose.

"You bettah put that down 'fore sumbody gits hurt." Sarah sassed back. Suddenly, Mountain girl pride was on the line here. The Hatfields and McCoys never looked this good dressed up.

Sarah dropped her hands on her hips, and one slowly jutted to the side.

Bring it — She dared her. She lowered her head until she was peeking through her bangs. The two stared each other down.

Sarah tried, but couldn't hold a straight face, and the laughter dam burst wide open. The crew members were sure they had lost their minds. Work went on around them as they sank into quicksand silliness. They peered around to see if anyone would notice their giggle-fit.

Hanah whispered, "Oh, they ain't payin' us no never-mind."
Sarah snorted, and the giggle-fit started all over.
Finally, they collected themselves, and Sarah spoke up.

"I couldn't help but see his wrist. What happened?" Sarah was genuinely curious.

"He was playing baseball, got hurt and broke it. A couple of days later, in a cast, that boy, bless his heart, went back out and done it again." Hanna sighed heavily. This was the first time Sarah recalled any emotion from her.

"I didn't have the money to fix it proper, so they did the best they could, but it's not quite right. That's why we moved here, near better specialists."

"He had to change schools, has had trouble making friends... and he gets teased terrible. His grades are slipping a bit. I am sure it'll all get fixed up. We need a little time to work it all out."

After another minute of taking in the whirlwind of activity in the hall, Hannah spoke up.

"How you, Shugah? Last night gave me the hamster mouth sumthin' awful this morning, Have Mercy." Hannah made a face that caused Sarah to snort again... *Even with that stank face, her sunshine came through.*

S o much happened in a week that Duncan lost track of everything. The woodwork gleamed; the lights were brightly polished. Different pieces of gear were all stored in their proper place. A new teleprompter sat in front of the Dais. Several cameras were placed in the room to capture everything that was happening.

It was a lot to take in, but Timmy assured Duncan he would help focus the message he was trying to convey. Tonight, it was the rehearsal for the opening of the facility.

Everything until then had been very old school, out in the field, under a tent. They moved inside when it was cold. A traveling ministry that didn't travel.

Drive-up Divinity — Timmy called it. Duncan resisted using a phrase like that and asked that others not do so either.

Service of others, in Their name. — If you say anything, that's what you call it. Duncan reminded them often of the saying Sarah lived by, an echo from her father.

Do the right thing. — Mr. Griffin's words were the notes that came from the Harp of Humanity.

Service of others, in Their name, by doing the right thing.

His pledge for tomorrow. The message will be loud and clear.

The rehearsal the night before went far easier than anyone expected. Nothing glitched, nothing crashed, and Duncan enjoyed strolling with his new wireless lavalier microphone. He preferred to walk while he talked. He occasionally stopped by the Dais to sip the water, but not to command attention. Wandering back and forth felt natural and comfortable.

But Duncan accepted, people didn't always want homey. They desired an edict, and it never wavered.

Service of others, in Their name, by doing the right thing.

The next day, while waiting to go out, he paced nervously. He glanced out at the parking lot, peeking through the blinds.

Totally full. Duncan rippled with fear. *How long before we have to add additional time slots?*

"Being outside is so different from this. At least out there, you can focus on everyone's faces." Duncan's remarks were to no one in particular. Sometimes he just needed the walls to listen. Alan came in and stopped a few feet from him. "Two minutes, Mr. Graham."

Well, that was a little formal — I guess it's time.

Timmy met him at the doors of the Vestry.

"Remember, when you are at the podium, look for messages on the teleprompter. Just do what it says. I've got everything handled, be Duncan Graham." Timmy reached under the back of Duncan's jacket and turned on the microphone pack.

Timmy spoke into his headset. "Cue walk-in music."

"Wait for the light to come through the door window. As soon as that happens, that's when you come out." Timmy gave Duncan his last set of instructions and disappeared down the side hall.

Headed for The Pilot House — Duncan laughed inside. What a name. Timmy said he was driving, so... let him drive.

Muffled sounds filtered through the walls and door. Suddenly, the small window lit up, casting a beam of light onto the ground.

Duncan closed his eyes, took a deep breath...

...and walked through the door.

For the next hour, Duncan told stories, related how he would do things around the neighborhood to help. How, as you grow up, you forget how to bring joy to others by doing for them.

You know, the feeling you have when walking away from having done something for someone else. Everyone knows that experience.

Heads nodded in agreement. He asked people to stand up and share how they practiced this. Everyone listened intently as wireless microphones found their way to those who shared their story. There were incidents of assisting an elderly neighbor, a young boy mowing the lawn across the street, and carting groceries in on a rainy day.

"No one likes to get wet when bringing the shopping in." Duncan (and most of the crew) imitated Hannah's *stank face.* It had become a running gag.

She does it best, though — Sarah caught Duncan trying to imitate it many times. Hannah giggled from the front row, Jacob sitting beside her.

It cain't be all bad iff'n that boy is imitating me. She was secretly flattered, blushing and bashful all at the same time.

Duncan walked back and forth, then he stopped at the Dais. It slowly rose, but it didn't bother him. He paused on purpose and surveyed the room. His image was up on several large screens. No one had a bad seat.

He started carefully, "You... me... everyone has something to share. Everyone of you."

He continued to survey the room.

"Each one of us here was in service to one other."

Another pause.

"You didn't even know it."

He sensed the cameras closing in on his face. You couldn't help but spot it in all the displays.

"You listened. You listened in silence. You were present. You paid attention."

"Sometimes, that is the hardest thing to do, day to day... but it is the most IMPORTANT thing to do." He picked up a message from the teleprompter.

Raise your hand to the left and say, Mrs. Jenkins. You'll know what to do next.

Duncan read the words twice, to be sure. — *Trust Timmy.*

Duncan shifted his gaze to the left, slowly raised his hand, and said, "Mrs. Jenkins?"

The lights came on over a group near where Duncan was looking. An older woman rose. A microphone quickly came to her. She was choking a wad of tissues in her hands. Swollen red eyes, empty and pleading, gazed at Duncan.

The Dais lowered, and Duncan moved off it, towards her.

"My.. My husband of 47 years recently passed." Her eyes welled up again. "And I am so alone. So afraid..."

People all around her reached out to comfort her.

"Do you feel that?" he gestured to the people surrounding her. Duncan wanted privacy however, so he yanked out the thin microphone cable. "If you are here, you are NEVER by yourself." He stepped into the aisle and walked to her row. He held out his arms to her.

This should be between her and me. Duncan felt... uncomfortable.

She slowly squeezed past people to stand in front of him. He had a tear running down his face. The cameras made sure it was on the screens.

He took her hands in his. "Don't be AFRAID." He waited a moment, and several spotlights came up on the two of them. "You...." Duncan's voice caught, briefly. "... will be fine."

Mrs. Jenkins glanced at Duncan and those surrounding her. "I.. I.. I have no fear." She was still holding the microphone handed to her, which broadcast the entire message in the Hall.

The crowd gasped. The beams of light disappeared. The music slowly swelled.

Duncan surveyed the faces and said, "Go and be of service to others. Others will be of service to you, I promise."

He kissed Mrs. Jenkins on the forehead. The people in her vicinity embraced her with love. Duncan listened as they promised to schedule cooking or card nights...

She needs people to recognize her and to be with her.

Sarah kept an eye on all this a few rows away. She looked on as Duncan made his way to the front of the room to greet everyone, like he always did.

With ease.

It didn't sit quite right with Duncan, and he was not the only one who picked it out.

———◆◇◆———

Chapter Eleven

D UNCAN PACED THE VESTRY like a caged animal.
His eyes darted around the room, looking for
some sense of what felt like a manufactured spectacle.
Sarah strode into the room. She glared at a Duncan she
had never seen before. The boat rocked too much for her
liking.

"Bring Timothy in here."

Duncan was never that abrupt or formal with that
name. *Something's wrong.* She went over everything she
sat through and couldn't put her finger on it. She sensed
something was off.

She found Timmy on the other side of the hall with
Alan. They were having a hushed conversation in a
corner. One look at her and they quickly stopped. Sarah
motioned for them to follow her. They stepped fast to
get to her side and moved back to the Vestry.

"Timothy, go find Duncan, NOW." She mirrored
how serious Duncan had been with her.

"What's the matter, Mu'um?" Alan asked. The concern in his voice hung like humidity on a hot day.

"We're staying here." Sarah pointed to the floor. Alan obliged with no questions or challenge.

Timmy pushed through the door. As soon as Duncan saw him, he launched into a rage.

"What the hell was that?"
What did you do?
"Was that a set-up?"
Was it all a show?

Timmy stood there. He expected a little pushback, but not a full-on carpet bombing.

"I DID NOTHING FOR THAT WOMAN. THE WARMTH? NOT THERE. I DIDN'T FEEL ANYTHING!"

The words were coming rapid fire.

Duncan continued to pace erratically.

The commotion carried through the walls. Everyone still in the Hall could sense the seismic meltdown that was happening. McKenna was in the Hall, talking with a few stragglers. She finished her pleasantries and headed straight for the ruckus.

The door in the Outer Vestry cracked open, and she

poked her head in. Sarah's attention was focused on the conversation happening inside, so she didn't notice anything. Alan quietly opened his palm at his side to stop her and shook his head ever so slightly. McKenna slinked back out of sight.

Within the Inner Vestry, the storm clouds were still thickening.

Duncan paused at the window and pulled back the curtains as if to let the sunlight burn him. He stopped pacing.

"Look at me." Timmy's words fell on deaf ears.

"LOOK at me." Timmy was not moving.

Duncan turned to glare at his firmest supporter. *How could he do this to me?*—Duncan's heart ached.

"Are you done? I mean, ARE YOU DONE? Are you ready to have a big boy conversation?" Timmy was suddenly the adult in the room.

"Don't EVER talk to me like that. EVER." Timmy drew a hard line, and Duncan was clearly over it.

By MILES.

"That woman left here different than when she walked in. In my book? That's a gift." He let the point sink in.

"The people around her all reached out. Another gift. People told stories about their selfless acts openly, and everyone listened. Gift. All day long." He paused again to make sure the point was getting across.

"All I did was make sure people witnessed that gift."

Duncan's eyes blinked incredulously.

"You wanna have a pity party, I'll be there with Kleenex. But this..." as he dramatically flailed his arms in front of Duncan, "...save the drama for your mama. I don't have time for THIS." He flailed his hands once more.

Duncan couldn't help it. He tried to stifle it, but he couldn't contain it. A laugh burst from his lips. He realized exactly how ridiculous he looked.

"You can have doubts and fears. If you didn't, I'd be worried."

Timmy handed him a cloth to wipe his face. He moved back, pretending to avoid stepping on something on the floor.

"Keep it off my shoes. Veronica would kill me."

Timmy and Duncan came through the inner Vestry

door. Apparently, detention was over.

"Are you two finished?" Sarah was a little miffed, arms folded across her chest, her hip jutting out to the side as she tapped her foot. These conversations should happen in private, and the fact that it happened in a very public place infuriated Sarah.

Timmy slinked by her, head down. Duncan stopped in front of her, trying to keep his head down in shame... but the giggles persisted.

She glared from one to the other.

"Duncan Graham, you KNOW we have somewhere to be tonight, and we are already late. I am never late. YOU are making me crazy. And HERE? You decide to melt down HERE? NOW?"

Timmy tried to contain himself. "YOU are not helping, Mister." She was fuming.

He stifled the giggling long enough to hear the exasperated breath escape Sarah's lungs.

It was HER turn to pace back and forth.

Her arms came up, flopped at her sides, and her head shook back and forth. She strode up to face Duncan, eyes squinting, focusing every laser beam her eyes could muster on him.

"It's like you are a snail…"
"…on the back of a turtle…"
"…walkin across…. arrrgh… quicksand!"

She realized she had a fistful of her dress on each side and was crushing the material like a plastic bottle. She was having her own volcanic moment.

Timmy and Duncan were doing everything they could to keep from losing their composure. They were horribly unsuccessful.

"If'in this dress gets any more wrinkled, I'll twist a knot in you, so hep me…" Sarah stared him down for a moment, then winked at him, a glint in her eye. The backwoods attitude was certainly loud and proud.

Duncan swatted her on the backside. "G'won now. Git"

You wanna sass me? Gimme some.
She hit Duncan with a side-eye. There might have been a smirk too. The tension level came down dramatically.

A moment passed, and Alan asked if they wanted him to drive. Duncan thanked him but said they were ok. People gathered items and prepped to go home. Off in a corner, Timmy and Alan got back into one of their deep conversations, away from prying ears.

"I told you, everything will be in place…" Sarah

overheard Timmy and Alan. They quickly shifted away from the group.

What are they up to? Sarah glanced over as they left the Vestry. They got in the car and pulled away. A few miles of silence was enough for Sarah.

"You gonna tell me what that was all about?" She asked. The sass was long gone.

"Is what happened today... is it... was it right?" Duncan stared at her with a quizzical look.

"You didn't feel it, did you?"

Duncan pondered for a moment.

"No."

"I could tell. You didn't act like you normally do when something happens. It scared me a little."

"Me too. And I didn't know how to handle it. I blamed Timmy." Duncan paused. Timmy's words made sense.

"That woman, when she left, had something that she didn't have when she came in. Maybe it's not always about me, but it's what's happening around me. I need to heed my own words and listen more."

"Hmm." Sarah pondered for a moment. The mountain girl started creeping back in.

Pick his spirits up. That's what he needs.

Sarah knew him better than anyone else . She decided that seriousness was not needed at the moment.

"Duncan Graham? Listen more? Serious?" Duncan peered over at her.

"I've been tellin' you I want a porch. For three years. Tellin'. You? Listenin'?" She muttered to herself, "...deaf as a rock   ...probably as old as one too..." She poked him in his side. He focused his eyes back out the windshield.

"I'm not listening. What about a torch?" He smirked.

Oh?

"Go find a pay phone. Find a pay phone and let me dial the number, then YOU ask your mama to see if you can sleepover," she fired back.

"Still not listening." He shot again.

Sarah's hand flipped up and totally dismissing his statement.

Duncan stared straight ahead, watching the lack of traffic in front of him.

While stopped. In a parking spot.
In front of Hannah's place.
And they were late for dinner.

"I'll wait all night, if you want me to." Duncan said, with a smirk.

Damn him — the goosebumps were on full display.

I t was a delightful dinner. Hannah made something from the backwoods cookbook: chicken and dumplings.

My pawpaw teach'd me how—Sarah couldn't resist her back home sayings and accent.

"Those poor boys back home have no idea what they missed," Sarah told Hannah over dessert. The girls sat back, relaxed and watched over their boys off in the corner.

Jacob talked about school and working on a science project about 'Photosynthesis'. Duncan and Jacob sat there talking about plants. The girls eyed them, sipping their seemingly bottomless glasses of wine.

"That boy," Hannah admitted, "will be the death of me. There's only so much I cain do wit him when we go to the park. He needs to be wi' other proper boys his age."

"I figgur I bout' be right lined up to git him to that specialist ovah in Jackson County to check his wrist."

Sarah asked, "Can it be fixed?"

"They tell me they can fix it right up, but he'll hafta go to therapy to git his strength back. I dunna wanna think 'bout what might happen if it doesn't work. That boy don't need no mo' sufferin'." Hannah stared deep into her wineglass. Her lip trembled as she looked up at Sarah, her eyes moist.

"Jus being around you and your family has hep'd him so much. He's out of his shell, and they's always findin thangs for him to do. They don't treat him like he's different, like they do in school."

Hannah gazed at the two of them sitting in the corner, with Jacob practicing his project speech. Duncan sat, listened, and asked questions, making suggestions where Jacob might improve a little. Sarah walked over and leaned against the wall.

I think I need to help things along.

Sarah stood in the hallway, looking at them.

"Jacob, did you know that Dun, um, Mr. Graham played baseball like you? What was it, second base?" Sarah led the conversation off.

"Really? I was a shortstop!" Jacob perked up. Baseball got him excited more than free ice cream.

"Yeah, but I wasn't any good, but I had fun. You know, Mr. Anderson?"

"You mean Timmy? He won't let me call him Mr. Anderson."

"We played ball together since we were about your age."

"My team won a league championship, and I got a big trophy. C'mere, I'll show yah."

Jacob and Duncan got up and headed to the bedroom. As Duncan passed Sarah, she grabbed his pinky with hers.

"Y'all LISTEN to that boy," Sarah implored.

Duncan nodded slowly. Hannah got up from where she sat, being protective but curious at the same time.

Sarah stood in the corridor, and Hannah moved in behind her. "You know, he gets real depressed about that sometimes, not playing any mo'."

Sarah glanced over her shoulder and said, "You have to trust me."

Hannah searched her eyes. She felt safe with Sarah, and that is something she had lost long ago.

She kissed Sarah on the cheek and meekly said, "I do."

The boys were busy talking and laughing when the girls tiptoed down the hallway. They stayed out of sight for the moment.

"There are so many trophies! Holy Moley! And this picture of you, in that uniform? What team was that for?"

"That was for the Birch River Baptist Baseball squad. We played at other churches in the area. Wasn't a lot of places to play ball in the mountains, but plenty of kids. We won one year, and that's where that trophy came from."

"One time I got most improved out of the WHOLE league!" His smile faded a bit.

The girls were in the bedroom's doorway now, and Hannah tried to push through to her son. Her protective instincts were kicking in, but Sarah stopped her.

"Wait," she begged. She grabbed Hannah's right arm and pulled it over her shoulder. She pulled Hannah close.

Hannah got closer and hugged Sarah from behind and rested her chin on Sarah's shoulder.

"We got here, and I wanted to play, but no one wanna take a chance on someone like me. I wish they would..." His shoulders drooped ever so slightly. "...but I am still the team manager!"

Duncan studied all the trophies. The passion was everywhere.

"Well, why don't you show them what you can do?" Duncan asked.

The boy looked away. The smile totally disappeared. He turned back to Duncan and asked, "You don't know?"

Duncan said, "Know what?"

Hannah's hand was on Sarah's arm, just above the elbow. She buried her face in Sarah's shoulder and squeezed her arm.

Jacob focused on his right hand. He always wore long sleeves to hide it. He held out his arm and slowly pulled the sleeve up.

The joint had a huge bump, and the wrist bone was out of place. He quickly tried to cover it up. Duncan stopped him.

"Is this why they tease you?" Duncan never understood why differences made people act the way they do.

"I got hurt at a game and they fixed it, but I didn't listen to my Mom. I went out before I should, and played more. I just wanted to play. Hurt it more and we couldn't have it fixed right. And that's all my fault."

Duncan recognized the sadness in Jacob's eyes. Hannah was sobbing. She hid her face on Sarah's shoulder. Duncan felt the sorrow ripple through him.

Hannah's pain barricade sprang a leak. Anguish rippled through the opening.

"I broke my mama's heart. That's why I don't get into trouble no more. She didn't deserve for me to be stupid."

There was no mistaking it. The pull. It guided Duncan's hands. It gave him a voice.

Duncan put his hand on Jacob's head. "Neither do you. Close your eyes for a minute. I promise it will be alright."

Sarah lifted Hannah's head, her eyes, puffy and red from crying.

Duncan asked Jacob to give him the wrist. Jacob's

own barricade trickled. Duncan's hands were drawn to Jacob's wrist.

Do not ignore the pull when it calls to you... Unspoken, but the words echoed in Duncan's ears.

The warmth built and flowed through him. Hannah noticed Sarah's goosebumps—then they passed into her as well.

What—

"Turn your wrist over."

"I can't."

A light filled the room. You wanted to shield your eyes, but didn't have to.

"Jacob Cassidy, turn your wrist over. You're fine."

The light dissipated. Jacob stared at his hand. He was holding a ball. He hadn't done that in years.

"MOMMA?"
He couldn't believe what he was seeing. His eyes widened while his mouth fell open.
"MOMMA? LOOK!"

Tears of joy streaked Jacob's face. Tears of relief glistened on Hannah's.

Hannah pushed past Sarah and fell to her knees in front of Jacob. She blessed herself, focused on Jacob, "Oh baby. My baby!" She was crying in Jacob's arms. Jacob held her and let her cry.

Sarah moved to help Duncan up. His legs wobbled, and he struggled to rise. Sarah put an arm around him and steadied him.

Duncan looked back at Jacob, and they exchanged glances. Both Hannah and Jacob were sobbing.

Sarah and Duncan left the room and closed the door.

Chapter Twelve

A COUPLE OF WEEKS slipped quietly away since that night with Jacob.

Hannah hadn't been by as much because she was carting her boy to specialists to understand what happened. Sarah was quietly footing the bill. She couldn't come right out and explain it to her yet. She wanted Hannah to make sure the doctors said that her boy was really okay to start doing more.

Let her come along slowly.

Events at the church were still happening, but settled into a groove Duncan could tolerate. He grew to regard the extras as something that helped keep people's focus on the message.

Sometimes, he manifested the gift, but when he didn't, he learned to pivot and turn to those around him to lean in and be present.

It covered a LOT of little idiosyncrasies.

"I guess it's okay to have an off day." Duncan treated it like it was a sport.

Oh, I didn't hit the fastball today.

Oh, I hit a home run today.

Oh, I hit for the cycle with a Grand Slam.

One day, at one of the gatherings, a cameraman didn't pay attention to where the camera was pointed. A teleprompter message was broadcast to all the screens (and the new local TV feed), clear as day. *To your right. 2nd row. William, in a yellow shirt.*

There was a swirl of questions in the town paper and talk amongst the 'flock'.

What was the reason for this?
Why would you need to know this?
How did you find this information?
Do they have people planted in the group?
How much of this is real?

Every statement Duncan tried to make was twisted, wrongly quoted, or the answer was already written before the interview. People came out of the woodwork claiming to have attended one of the meetings, but nothing happened to them personally.

Or worse, something did happen, but whatever it was, it didn't last.

Some people whom Duncan helped wouldn't say that it was anything he did.

One day, a group showed up at the hall and protested. They called themselves The Doubters. One of them had been helped by Duncan, but he couldn't bring himself to believe. They carried signs, protested outside the hall and made a general nuisance of themselves. The coverage was all over the news.

Sarah had plenty of nights where she was nursing her own doubts about herself and having to prop up Duncan at the same time. It was exhausting for them both. The world they lived in was peeling away little by little. All of the fantastic, wonderful support they received was drying up.

Duncan was forced back to work part-time at Blair's shop, but stayed out back. He didn't want to be recognized and have it hurt her business.

On a busy morning, he was unpacking a delivery when he saw Alan pull up, pop out of the car and head over to talk to McKenna. He had never known him to come by the garden center. He had only seen him at the Hall, or at the pub. McKenna's head bobbed in acknowledgement as Alan was talking. He turned as if to head inside, but McKenna stopped him. Alan tried to catch a glimpse inside, but then turned back to her. They embraced for a moment, and Alan drove off.

Duncan thought back to the Hall. On the day the protesters came, it was Alan who went to speak to them and ask them to leave peacefully. However, it was only after a long conversation with one of them, during which both cast glances back at the window to the Vestry.

He talked to many people on the inside... and some on the outside.

What was he up to?

He was ALWAYS nearby when something was happening, either good or bad. He was in the middle, but was he helping or hurting?

Did we do this wrong?
Did I really do anything worthwhile?
I can't remember the last time I...

Duncan's self-doubt was worse than the stories others made up.

A lot of quiet nights passed. The ringing phone pierced a cool fall night.

"Oh, hi, Hannah! Sarah's right here." Duncan handed the receiver over to Sarah. Their hands touched.
Nothing. No goosebumps. Nothing. She ached for that feeling again.

"Hannah! How's things?" She listened for a minute.

"Tomorrow night, sure, I can come by. Ohhh, I miss you too. Around 6?" She turned to check with Duncan, and he nodded in agreement.

It'll be good for her to get away from me for a night.

"Okay, I will! Yes, I'll bring a bottle of wine too. Bye." She hung up the phone and walked behind Duncan in the chair. She placed her hands on his shoulders and leaned over and bussed the top of his head.

"That's from Hannah." Duncan smiled and put his hand over Sarah's. He gazed up at her, then took her hand and kissed it.

"You two will have a lot of catching up to do. I'm so glad you are getting together."

Duncan's smile was easy, friendly and warm. She adored that he was still holding her hand. Surprised, she scanned her arm.

I can still feel them. The goosebumps. Not gone... yet.

The next night, Sarah arrived right at 6 o'clock. Two wine glasses already sat filled on the table. A candle burned nearby. The potpourri was simmering on the stove.

Oh, it's going to be one of THOSE nights.

She needed one.

"Where is he?" she inquired about Jacob.

"Honey, you bettah sit down," Hannah said. She relayed her son was older now, and, well, he still loved Sarah, but he had to be realistic and confessed that he really liked someone in his class named Bobbi.

"I'm crushed! I can't compete... with a Bobbi! Even the name is adorable." Sarah squealed. She remembered her first crush from years ago... but not his name.

"You're crushed? That's mah baby! He's not supposed to like anyone till I'm old and droop like a dawg's ears."

Oh my gawd, that will NEVER happen to you — Sarah couldn't come up with that mental image.

For the next few hours, the laughs came easily, like time stood still. Jacob was excelling in school and started playing sports again. His confidence was soaring and was really getting into horticulture and was thinking of becoming a Botanist.

Sarah was so excited about their good luck. Duncan loved to work with the plants, so they connected easily. She thought back to where they had met, at Blair's greenhouse. Hannah brought Jacob there to meet Blair, and she was always ready to teach, so Jacob fit right in.

"Yes, she's well, and so is McKenna," Sarah shared.

Back and forth it went. Before you knew it, the first bottle vanished. They knew they shouldn't, but another snuck up on them.

Hannah delicately asked about the Hall and Duncan. She caught wind of all the nasty rumors and questions, and she didn't want to bring anything down on Jacob.

Sarah relayed that Duncan was struggling; he had doubts about himself and what he had done or tried to do. She confessed that their relationship had changed.

"I don't know if I am in love with him or with the attention, and I hate myself for it."

Sarah took a long, protracted breath.

"He's never given me a reason to doubt him, but I find all my worst fears from my past keep coming to the surface."

"That man is precious. That man, chil', is a pillar. Blinders on to anything BUT you."

She took a sip from her glass and continued.

"I've thrown th' sexy side-eye at him and it just bounces off."

In all these years, that is the first grain of vanity you have ever had. It made her more endearing to Sarah. *She knows she's beautiful and doesn't even pull that bullet out of the holster.*

"There isn't a man on this planet who would turn away from you. If they did, I'd take them to the Emergency Room—because something's *clearly* wrong with them," Sarah said, just stating the truth.

Hannah looked her dead in the eyes and said, "Girl, that man is blind in one eye and deaf in the other, outside of you. You walk off a cliff, he's gunna fall faster and catch you at the bottom. You do not need to worry about that boy at all. Period. End of sentence. End of Chapter. Put the book away, say yer prayers, turn off the light and get thee to sleep."

Sarah believed in her resolve. *But why can't I be that strong? Unwavering?*

"You're right. I trust him. It's me that's broken. I can't get my head around the what if and get it out of my brain..."

Hannah took another sip of wine. Her heart ripped open at Sarah's confession.

That kind of pain left a mark that was hard to remove, and Hannah knew it firsthand. She had to stop Sarah's doubt. The girls sat in silence for quite some time. One could accept everything in front of her. One couldn't.

F all faded away to Winter. The snow covered the troubles for a short time, but then came Spring. Nature crept forward. The residents of James Bend tried to do the same.

Now that Jacob started playing baseball again, Duncan attended games often. Jacob loved hearing him there, cheering him on from the fence by the dugout. Duncan made sure he got a spot super close.

Occasionally, he would drop Sarah off with Hannah and take Jacob to the game, filling up on 'man' time. With a cap and his new haircut, he fit in without anyone recognizing him.

Sarah hated the look. She understood why he did it, for a fresh 'beginning', but she admitted to Hannah, on one of their wine-filled nights...

I miss grabbing a handful of hair and planting a big one on his goofy face.

"So, work with whatch'all got, girl. That boy won't fight yah." Hannah was clearly a cheerleader in their corner.

Early spring in the Bend was a mixture of aromas in the air. Fresh-cut grass, Lilac blossoms and Magnolia trees all mixed. If the breeze tickled your nose from another direction, it'd be all different scents.

Someone baking bread, maybe a backyard grill or a fire pit.

And if it wasn't the fragrance that hit you, the colors would make you think you wandered into a room full of spilt rainbow paint. Blair always had a broad palette to choose from at the Garden Center, and this year was just as diverse.

She expanded into landscape planting services, and her crews were busy all over The Bend, sowing, sprucing and keeping up her Better Homes and Gardens "Americana Neighborhood" award.

One early summer day, Duncan passed by the duplexes that had been built a few years ago. It took a bit for the neighbors to accept them, but they filled quickly, and with decent families. It had been a while since the 'scandal', and people ignored him now.

Scandal schmandal. They don't believe in the good they did.

Duncan resigned to let them live with what they did to themselves.

He bounced up the steps and rang the doorbell to Hannah's duplex. She was lucky and didn't have a neighbor, so it was basically hers.

The door opened with Hannah's big smile front and center. It hardly ever left her face.

She's a walking ad... For toothpaste or a dentist.

She stepped aside, and he walked in.

"Is Jacob ready? I'm here to go with him to his game."

"Your girl didn't tell you? He is riding with his coach today. He is already gone."

"Oh." They had barely crossed paths that morning.

Musta slipped her mind — he didn't think anything of it.

Hannah sat on one of the counter stools she had at her breakfast nook. She knew she hadn't told Sarah about Jacob riding with the coach.

"Y'all ok? I mean, we d'int have a chance to talk a lot and thangs got real spicy there for a Mountain Minute." Hannah was curious.

He gazed down at the linoleum, embarrassed. "Well, I haven't giv.."

"Duncan," Hannah's voice changed. It was soft. It was... alluring.

He peeked up from the floor.

Hannah was looking right at him, biting her lower lip slightly. Her fingers hovered over the first button of her blouse. Her hands trembled.

Go ahead. Go on. Settle this once and for all. Hannah glanced away for a second, then back at Duncan.

She wasn't trying to flaunt her beauty.
She didn't want him to say yes.
She just wanted to show Sarah *no, needed* to prove he would say no.

Duncan turned away from her perfectly tanned skin.

"You did something amazing for me and my boy... I never..." She cast her eyes down at her shoes and back at Duncan, her lips parted as she exhaled slowly.

He'll stop me; I know it.

Duncan, struck silent, weighed what was happening right in front of him. It wasn't even a question of what to do. He needed to do it gently.

Hannah nervously fumbled with the buttons. She already had three undone.

"Do you..."

Duncan shuffled towards her. Now close to the barstool, he looked at Hannah, his hands taking hers away from her top.

After a moment of looking directly into her eyes, he started to re-button her shirt.

"This is something that doesn't serve either of us."

Hannah closed her eyes. Inwardly, relief washed over her.

Duncan finished buttoning her blouse. He wiped a single tear from the corner of her eye. He stepped forward and hugged her.

Her head drooped, not in shame but in embarrassment.

I knew he couldn't be tempted, but I still... tried. What is wrong with me? Why would I do that?

Guilt and humiliation steamrolled her at the same time.

I even wore a skin-colored tank top under my shirt so nothing would happen. Why do I feel guilty?

Duncan took a step back and stared at Hannah. He nodded slightly, as if everything was okay.

It's NOT okay. It's NOT.

Duncan turned around, side-stepping to the front door and opened it.

He muttered, "It's okay," and walked out the door.

Hannah had to tell Sarah. She snatched her jacket from the chair and headed out the back door, through the woods, towards Sarah's place. The branches and twigs snapped under her feet as she dashed through the woods.

She was breathless when she reached Sarah's house, so she stood there in the backyard for a moment to collect herself.

She'll understand. Go slow. You did nothing wrong.

H annah took one more deep breath, twisted the doorknob, and sauntered in. Nothing out of the ordinary, she came over often and just wandered in.

"Hey Sunshine!" Hannah said. Sarah's head came around with a big smile.

"Aren't you as sweet as Grandma's Tea! C'mere and gimme some love."

They hugged in the middle of the kitchen. Sarah

stepped back and went right into the refrigerator to fetch her own homemade lemonade. "I just made this, what perfect timing."

She set it on the table and moved to grab two glasses.

"None for me, baby."

Be gentle.

Hannah moved and sat at the table. She flicked the end of a sugar packet with her fingernail. She stared at the packet and searched for the right words.

"Remember when we talked about how people sometimes don't seem to be who you think they are?"

Sarah sat down and nodded.

"Well, I wanted to... um."

"What?" Sarah leaned in. She ran her hand down Hannah's trembling forearm.

"It was all supposed to be..."

Something wasn't right. The hair on the back of Sarah's neck stood up. "What? What was it supposed to be?"

"I told you about my ex and how he t'weren't nothin like I prayed for..." Hannah couldn't look at Sarah.

"Spit it out." Sarah hissed. She didn't realize she was standing. She was hovering over Hannah.

"Duncan came over today. I... I had already arranged a ride for Jacob... so I was there alone."

"You... what?"

"I was careful, I..."

"WHAT?"

"I was unbuttoning my blouse, and... and, but... underneath was..."

Sarah exploded. Years of rage surfaced in an instant.

"To me? You DID THIS to me? ME?"

Hannah began to cry and pleaded, but Sarah was having no part of it.

"After all we gave you? After all *I* did for you????"

Hannah was weeping. The emotional levee had been swept away.

"NOOOO Duncan... Dunc.." She couldn't force the words out between her sobs. She reached for Sarah's hand.

"Don't TOUCH me," Sarah lashed out as she walked away.

I SHOULD HAVE SEEN IT COMING. WHY WAS I SO STUPID? The phrase burned in her head.

Sarah spun on her heels and faced the table. Makeup and tears streaked Hannah's face.

"Out," Sarah said, with a scary calmness. Hannah put her hands over her face, trying to hide it. *I've ruined everything. She meant everything to me, and I destroyed it.*

"I said, *Get Out.*" Sarah marched over to the back door and opened it. Hannah searched for something she knew she would never find.

Sarah Griffin.

Her friend. A partner in crime. Someone who felt her soul.

That person left on the rage bus.

Hannah staggered to the door. Sarah wouldn't meet her gaze.

Hannah stumbled down the small wooden steps. Her legs barely worked. The door slammed behind her.

Inside the house, Hannah heard an angry scream and things crashing in the kitchen.

Sarah screamed again.

A glass broke somewhere inside. Violently.

She looked back at the door. Sarah glared at her through the window, but Hannah didn't recognize the face. She had never seen this look before.

They stared at each other as the sunlight faded. Sarah turned away and didn't look back. Seeing her friend turn away obliterated what little light in her soul remained.

She pivoted on her heels in shame and wandered back to her house.

Dusk settled in over James Bend in more ways than one.

Duncan came home with no idea what he was walking into. Sarah had been brooding and burning for hours.

The flamethrower was topped off with jet fuel, and

the trigger woman gassed up with Moonshine.

The front door opened, and something shattered on the wall next to it. Duncan flinched and searched for where it came from.

There was Sarah, sitting on a stool. Luggage sat nearby and was packed. A purse, with keys hanging from it, sat on top of the suitcase.

"HOW COULD YOU DO THIS?????"

"FAWKING MEN. MY MOMMA FELL FOR IT. I FELL FOR IT. HANNAH, THAT WITCH, FELL FOR IT."

"I AM GLAD MOMMAS DEAD SO SHE DIDN'T HAVE TO HAVE HER HEART CRUSHED AGAIN. AT LEAST I CAN GO BACK TO BEING..."

"Sarah," Duncan stepped forward.

"YOU ARE NOT CHARMING YOUR WAY OUT OF THIS. THIS ISN'T YOUR MINISTRY YOU CAN SWEET TALK YOUR..."

"Sarah," Duncan took another step closer. "You've got it all..."

"DON'T YOU TELL ME. SHE ALREADY CAME OVER AND CONFESSED. JACOB WASN'T THERE. UNBUTTONING HER BLOUSE... SHE

COULDN'T EVEN SAY IT, BUT SHE DIDN'T HAVE TO."

"TIMMY'S NOT HERE TO SAVE YOU. BLAIR? MCKENNA? NOT HERE EITHER. THIS IS ALL YOU. ALL ON YOU. A MAN LIKE YOU TRICKED MY MAMA. DESTROYED MY DADDY. I SAW IT ALL. I SAW THE SIGNS. I IGNORED THE SIGNS."

"Hannah didn't..."

"FIGHT YOU OFF? WHY SHOULD SHE? DAMN PERFECT AND SHE TAKES MY MAN? SHE CAN HAVE YOU."

Duncan stopped. He could feel the warmth building. The pull was urging him to act. He could take it away.

His instincts kicked in; he had to let it come out. She had been holding it for so long. Let it burn. Wait for the ashes.

They stood silently facing each other. Her breath was raspy and full of anger. The pull squeezed Duncan tighter and tighter with her every breath.

Sarah had no more jet fuel left in her tank.

The back door flung open and crashed against the counter. Alan stepped inside. Duncan leered at him and then back at Sarah.

What are you doing here? Did you have a part in all this? — Duncan's mind raced. The pull disappeared.

Alan looked at the scene before him, spotted the luggage and grabbed Sarah's suitcase and bag and took them out the front door.

"Step aside, Duncan." There was no room for misunderstanding what Alan meant.

Sarah walked by Duncan defiantly. When she reached the door, she took off the Claddagh ring and put it into his hand. She locked eyes with him, and with a voice that was soaked with disappointment, said, "All you had to do was the right thing."

She pivoted and walked to the car. After a short word with Alan, she got in. She never looked back.

Alan walked around to the driver's side, peered over the roof back to Duncan.

He opened his door, got in and drove off.

Chapter Thirteen

D UNCAN WAS GUTTED. Everything he had known was ripped from him.

He wasn't the cause of any of it. He would have owned it. He would have stepped up. He would have taken the lashes for things he was responsible for.

After Sarah left, he had nowhere to turn, no one to talk to. Nothing to ground him.

He got in the beat-up Toyota he still had. The dealership had decided a few months ago that fronting him a car was not a good business choice. He drove straight to the only place he considered safe. Not Timmy's. Not McKenna's.

The Hall.

The very place where prayers and questions were answered.

The very place that had no prayers or answers for him tonight.

He still had the keys, but it was shut up tight. A poster on the window announced the fire sale date next month. Soon, it would all be gone.

Let the lawyers figure it out.

He put his key in the back-door lock. It was rusty, so he had to jiggle it a little.

Great. Just great.

It snapped off.

Sure, what else? What else you got for me?

He walked around to the Vestry side door. It unlocked the first time.

As he stepped in, he flipped a single switch, and one small track fixture came on across the room. Not bright, but enough to make out overturned chairs, things on the floor and cleaning rags scattered about.

There were dust-covered surfaces everywhere, and books were all over the place. Blair's carefully placed potted plants were all dying or dead. They hadn't been watered for months. Some of them appeared as if they had been kicked over in anger.

Duncan gingerly stepped closer to the light.

There before him was a photo in a beautifully ornate frame. Duncan picked it up, the dust swirling everywhere. Duncan blew off as much as he could.

Sarah

There they were, a picture of the two of them, in front of McKenna's house, the flowers all in full bloom. He remembered the day vividly. It was warm, and a slight breeze made the leaves on the trees sway, almost hypnotizing you. Bumblebees flew around you, gathering up all the pollen they could. They lay there for a long while watching nature's wonder.

Timmy snuck up and snapped it, and they didn't even know. They were both lost in their own world.

It doesn't even exist anymore.

He pulled up an overturned chair and sat, staring at the image.

All that I've been blessed with, and I can't fix this.

He didn't care. He tried to hold his emotions in check. He knew better.

Grief washed over him like the surf on the beach. You never know how high or how hard it will hit you. You don't know if there's an undercurrent. He wasn't getting wet, but he felt like he was being pulled under, nonetheless.

The waves of emotion kept battering him. He stood, walked to the table where the overturned plants lay scattered in the single beam of light. He put the picture down. It was like someone switched on the tsunami setting.

CRASH. The first wave hit.

CRASH. The second wave hit.

UNDERTOW. It pulled him under. He was gasping for air.

CRASH. Another wave hit.

Every wave cut deeper. The current pulled him further under.

He turned and faced the one floodlight beaming down on him. It was red, and he was right in the middle of its beam.

Look at me.

The tears soaked his cheeks and spilt onto his shirt.

CRASH. The waves were growing.

UNDERTOW. He was being dragged along the rocky bottom.

He cried out loud, "Look at me!"

His hands and arms rose to his sides, in line with his shoulders.

"LOOK AT ME!!!"

Agony contorted his face. His heart slammed against the inside of his chest.

He gripped his hair with both fists and pulled-anything to rip the anguish out of his mind.

Small clumps came away in his hands. Rivulets of blood traced along his contorted face.

Staggering forward, he walked right into an overturned table. A jutting leg ripped a piece of his shirt covering his ribs and jabbed at his side. Anger and pain let fly a string of profanities.

He burned.

He accepted that he deserved this.

His hubris brought him to this.

"WHO AM I?"

"WHAT AM I? **ALL I KNOW IS THIS!**"

Behind him, in the shadows, a shoot from an

overturned plant under his palms straightened. It grew ever so slightly upwards, towards his hand.

Why give me something I don't understand? I DON'T UNDERSTAND...

T he door flew open. A flashlight bathed him in cold white light. McKenna and Alan rushed into the room.

There he lay crumpled on the floor, bathed in sweat and blood, clothes ripped and soaked. Battered into the floor by an invisible force that had forsaken him.

"Glory be, child, we found you. No one knew where you wandered off to." Her worry was palpable. "Worried sick, I was."

Alan moved to support his cousin. Exhaustion racked his body. He had been there for 4 hours. His legs were unsteady, and he could barely speak. Alan picked him up, helping him to his feet. Covered in grime and sweat, he collapsed into his cousin's arms.

Alan guided him to McKenna's car and placed him in the front passenger seat. She flipped the switch off in the Hall and closed the door with a thud. Duncan's key was still in the lock. Twisting it, the lock latched. She pulled the key out and turned towards the car.

She got in the back, and Alan brought them back to McKenna's house.

In the Vestry, a single plant, lit from the street lamp outside, reached blindly to the sky.

———————◆○◆———————

Chapter Fourteen

D UNCAN SAT in the coffee shop.

A generic shop, in a generic strip mall on a generic street.

In it was one of those trendy caffeine-latte-froth nonsense places that was all the rage now. A mix of earthy, crunchy granola meets addiction fed by drink, either hot or cold. Cool trendy colors on the wall, funky lights hanging from the ceiling, and constant ear-battering noise.

And refreshment available in seconds!

Well, maybe minutes. He swirled his beverage in the Styrofoam cup. He couldn't decide if he was hip... or hopeless.

Peering over the top edge of his laptop, he watched the chaos of the afternoon after-school crowd as they got their swirled caffeination fix. He looked back down at his screen and took a sip of his own fuzzy choco-java concoction.

Damn hypocrite.

He put the cup down and focused on the lesson spreadsheet.

You bow down before the same Dark Roast Deity the rest of them do.

Duncan picked up a stack of papers. Written across the tops, in various handwriting, were the names of students. He shuffled through them quickly to make sure there was something on each of the pages other than a scribble.

They are clever like that. Or lazy.

Duncan's world had morphed over the years. James Bend slowly aged out of its Americana feel and descended into the fast lane cookie-cutter suburbia that it had carefully avoided for so many years. The early families were old now, and the younger families didn't have the same community goals anymore.

Many had moved on.

Timmy and Veronica got married. Duncan learned they had a child.
That must have been 10, maybe 12 years ago.

A lot of the families went in different directions. Almost like a wind blew the seeds off a dandelion in a yard. Everything scattered.

The fire sale had raised enough money to cover all of its bills and have a little extra for Duncan to go back to school and eventually earn a teaching certificate. The only relic of the past was a single plant Blair found while cleaning. She repotted it and gave it to Duncan to put in his apartment.

That was a different world back then. It's a different world now.

Duncan didn't think of the past. He avoided anything that might remind him of that time. It was like a wound that had never healed. Best to avoid thinking about 'it'. He turned that switch off long ago.

He had been mindlessly flipping through the pages. The name stared back up at him. Somebody struck him with a sledgehammer.

Duncan.

Duncan Marshall-Stallings.

How did I not catch this in classes the first week of school?

Duncan struggled to recall a face. He sees a ton of new kids every year. Could it be? It was too coincidental.

Great. Just great. I'm never going to leave it behind.

Still, he couldn't help but be tickled that this might be Jamie's son.

It all flooded back. He closed his eyes and let it have its time, like a movie, in his head. It's easier to be detached if you imagine it's somewhere else with different characters.

Timmy and Veronica had moved. Blair met a wonderful man and remarried. They lived in the same house for years. McKenna moved to an over-55 community that had an attached assisted living facility.

Duncan was not a fan of that decision at all.

The last time he visited his mother, she told him that Alan was eventually moving back to Scotland, saying something about 'having done what he needed to do.' McKenna didn't really talk much more about her nephew.

They were both there after finding Duncan in the Hall that night, but it was a blur as to what happened after. People were around, checking in... a lot of voices... but that part of his memory was wiped clean.

Well, partially, but most of it was smudged well enough not to be recognizable.

He completed his certificate training and got a job in a local school district. Started as a substitute and worked up to a full-time teacher within two years. They paid for the remainder of the classes he needed to be appropriately accredited.

Something that's all mine. All earned. And NO crowds.

No crowds.

That's precisely what he needed. No pressure to be whatever it is they wanted. No expectations other than what he did in the last 5 minutes. In a crowd, he blended.

"Dunc?"

Another daydream ruined. Damn.

"DUNC?"

Duncan peeked up from his papers. He might have been older, but there was no mistaking who it was.

"Heeey!" Duncan answered with a light smile.

"Haaay!" Timmy shot back.

Just like that, they slipped back into a gentle current that had never gone away, just maybe dried up a bit.

Or forgotten. Duncan was glad to see him.

After getting a drink, Timmy came back and settled in across the table. "What are you doing around here?

Didn't you move upstate?"

"Yeah, I am back to finish up a few tasks and some business for my mom before she moves."

"Where is she going? I didn't think she'd ever leave The Bend."

"Hawaii. They lucked into a place; she's earned plenty of money, and she wants to be somewhere she can garden all year long."

"That's great. Tell her we bumped into each other, and I send her my love."

"I will. What's up with you?"

In the next hour, they talked about everything from his teaching job to leading everyday lives, to people in the past, and what had been happening.

Duncan spoke of McKenna's new living arrangement. The years were chipping away at things that would never last.

"I don't know where they ended up. Either of them." Timmy volunteered. Duncan didn't remember asking.

"Me neither. Hannah didn't deserve any of this, but I never reached out to her, and I probably should have. I don't know." Duncan was fighting his usual demons.

Should Have. Didn't. Call her. No. Apologize. For what? Hannah? Sarah???

He knew it would never leave him. He could only manage to keep it buried.

Duncan sensed Timmy was pausing. They never got like that. Not the two of them; they were always go, go, go. He squirmed in the silence.

"Dunc, I can't believe I ran into you here. You're the last person I expected to bump into."

"I..., you know, Ronnie and I had a girl; she's 11 now."

Another lapse. Duncan felt a tinge.

"She's having some difficulties that I don't wanna talk about in here, too public... and..."

Another hesitation, then a deep breath.

"I need a favor from you. Remember when we were kids? Back when I was sick?"

That was a LONG time ago.

"You used to still play with me. It didn't matter how bad I was; you always had something for us to do."

Who is tugging my shirt?

"I did a few things differently. It was nothing. You have done plenty for me that I couldn't do. That's why we're friends." Duncan wasn't catching on.

Timmy did not want to push.

"Do you remember when we were alone in my bedroom? You... you did something... and.. all these years, I've seen you do amazing things... and they happen all around you..."

Duncan tried to recall. He had vague memories of Timmy being sick, but nothing stuck out.

"One day we were spreading some mulch outside in your Mom's yard, remember?" he asked.

MULCH.

MULCH.

Something grabbed Duncan and yanked him forward.

A flood of memories came back. Mulch, helping him home... going over the next day...

Why was I crying?

Duncan remembered begging Timmy to get up —The light.

THE LIGHT...

"Did I do something to you????" Duncan asked in a panic.

"You really don't remember?"

Duncan clouded over, unsure. He searched Timmy's eyes.

"You..." Timmy was stunned. "... You... healed me."

He couldn't believe Duncan didn't remember.

"We were so young, but you did it. It was you and me." Duncan's jaw locked—nothing but silence.

It all made sense now. Timmy's loyalty. He did everything for me.

That's why he believed in me. And all this time I didn't recognize it!

Shame came over him. He buried his face in his hands.

"I am so SORRY. I can't understand why I was so blind to why you did all those things for ME."

"I never put it together. You didn't have to do it, but you did, and I gave you nothing back."

"I BELIEVE in you." Timmy was dead serious.

I DID NOTHING.

Timmy used Duncan's own message against him in the most loving way possible.

"Be of service to others..."

Timmy's words hung in the air like a sign above a store.

Be of service to others.. Is it...... you think it's that easy?

Duncan had never really listened to what he asked of others.

"...Anyway, could you come by Bends Medical? Ronnie and I are there with my girl... and..."

He could only hope something would spur Duncan.

TUG.

Timmy slowly finished, "...could you come by and see her? And Ronnie would love to see you, too."

It was faint... but it was there—The Pull. Duncan hesitated.

"I.. I don't do that anymore. Not for years. I haven't tried..."

Timmy's disappointment creased his face.

"I can't say if anything would happen, is all."

The feeling grew stronger. Duncan looked around. He was sure someone was pushing him.

Timmy spied his cup, which had been empty for a while. He crushed it, took it to the trash bin, and then came back to the table.

"And," Duncan continued, deflecting as hard as he could.

"I gotta finish up these papers tonight. I have to go out of town in the morning for a three-day teacher conference I can't miss."

I believed in you.

The air escaped from inside his lungs.

After gazing out the window, he worked up the courage to speak.

Timmy stood above him and stuck out his hand.

"Dunc, it was so good to run into you. Have a safe trip." He turned on his heels with a finality that scared Duncan.

The pull would not let him go. *It yanked at him. He couldn't breathe.*

"Timmy!" He bolted upright out of his chair.

Timmy stopped and cocked his head towards Duncan.

"I'll be there as soon as I land. Come straight from the airport."

The pull faded away.

Timmy caught his breath.

"It'll be okay. I'll be there."

Chapter Fifteen

A FTER HE LANDED, Duncan got in one of the hotel courtesy vans and headed for the Convention Center. He was among 1000 other teachers, signing up for workshops and classes.

Funny, the teachers are coming to learn how to teach.

He studied the faces; they all blended. No one stood out. No one paid any attention to him standing in the middle of the Center floor. He glanced at his program.

Understanding Differences: Teaching Teens. 11 am, upstairs, Conference Room 4.

The escalators looked like overflowing sardine tins. He glimpsed to his left that an elevator door was open. Two people got off, and one got on. He sprinted for the opening.

"Hold the door!"

He slithered in next to a woman in her 60s. She had an old-school marm shell to her.

"I hate elevators. So uncomfortable, but I hate crowds on the stairs more." You didn't have to guess how *she* felt.

"What floor?" she asked, with her finger ready to push a button.

"Um, four, I think." Duncan replied.

She pushed four on the panel and then 7.

"I'll get to the top and the damn thing will collapse, you'll see." She was crotchety.

Nooo doubt. Duncan fixed his eyes straight ahead.

"Damn thing, so slow."

Wow. WOW. I hope she's a hidden administrator. Duncan looked everywhere but towards her.

KLUNK
The elevator shook.
KLUNK

It jolted again. She clutched the handle, running around the elevator car. It was an instant white knuckle reaction.

"Yousee—itsgoingtocrash.—Iknewit—weregonnadieeee"

Zero to panic in 2 seconds flat.

"I am sure it's okay."

She started hyperventilating.

No, she's really worked up. Say something. Say it now. Talk her down.

Duncan gently laid his hand on her shoulder and spoke calmly.

"It's okay. It's nothing. We're fine."

Suddenly, her breathing slowed. Her tension disappeared. Her shoulders relaxed. The elevator stopped and opened on the 4th floor, and Duncan stepped forward.

He turned back for a moment.

"Are you okay? Want me to ride up to 7 with you?" he asked. He wanted to be sure she was calm.

"No, like you said..." She paused for a sec. As the door closed, she finished, "I'm fine."

Duncan stood there for a minute and watched the doors close. The numbers flashed and went up to 7, where it stopped.

Did I.... Nah.

He took a step, no weakness in his legs.
Nope.

The next two days were uneventful, but he couldn't shake the woman in the elevator. Focusing on seminars was impossible when he had his own questions to answer.

Is it even working? More than once, he stared at his hands as if they belonged to someone else.

But there was no warmth. No light. No after effects.

Nothing.

He headed back to the airport, caught his flight home and landed, where he sprinted to the taxi stand.

He had a promise to keep.

———————◆O◆———————

Chapter Sixteen

T HE TAXI FROM the airport to the Medical Center was excruciatingly long. The driver tried to engage Duncan in some conversations, but all he got were grunts.

Well, not the Duncan I remember—the cabbie pondered to himself.

Duncan didn't care that he was recognized. He was beyond that now. Most of the people who would care aren't in the area anymore. He stared out the window almost the whole way there. Nothing was the same.

Picket fences gave way to parking lots and convenience stores. Fast-food joints crowded out home-cooked meals in kitchens.

"We are powerless to stop the march of time. HA! Progress? Where?" Duncan muttered under his breath.

They drove up to the front of the medical center. The cabbie put it in park and shut off the meter.

"$24, please, Mr. Graham."

What? How do you know my name?

He yanked out two $20 bills out of his wallet and handed them forward. "Keep the change."

The cabbie came around and opened Duncan's door. As he slid out, Duncan caught the hack license with a picture on it out of the corner of his eye.

Reginald Brown

REGINALD BROWN?

Duncan exited the cab and took a shocked step back. The cabbie reached out his right hand to shake Duncan's. That's when he caught it.

The scar on his finger.

"Good to have you in my taxi, Mr. Graham. Have a great day," Reggie said as he got back in the cab. He put it in gear and pulled away, leaving Duncan's suitcase, and jaw, firmly on the ground.

Little known to Duncan, but Reggie had a few run-ins with the law and had been incarcerated. Earned his GED in jail and became the manager at the town limo and taxi company.

He stood for a second, trying to grasp the reality in

front of him.

Maybe I'm not supposed to understand.

He side-stepped to his right and walked in through the automatic doors of the main entrance. He strolled to the information kiosk while looking around.

A gift shop. How cute.

A coffee stand? I guess the nurses needed to caffeinate.

A seating area. Why would anyone want to sit in here?

He spotted several portraits on the wall.

James Bend Benefactors

There it was.

Blair Anderson

Duncan recognized her, even without his glasses on. He stared for a minute before turning to the people behind the reception desk.

Name? "Graham."

Seeing? "Timothy Anderson."

The clerks exchanged glances.

How did this person know Mr. Anderson was here today?

One of the clerks stood up and folded his arms across his chest.

"Are you family?" The clerk asked. Seemed more like an interrogation to Duncan.

"Yes, and he is expecting me. Where can I find him?" Duncan was a little firmer in his questioning.

"He's either in Records filling out paperwork." The clerk paused, peering sideways at his desk partner.

"Or he is downstairs, one floor," the second attendant finished.

"In the morgue."

The iciness in her voice froze the blood in Duncan's veins. He turned and sprinted to the stairway, forgetting his luggage at the desk. He instinctively threw himself down the stairs and burst through the door, down one floor.

In the hallway in front of him were several doors leading to the places that Hospitals want to hide. He walked down the corridor, reading the room names stenciled on the doors.

Billing No.
Records No.
Phlebotomy No.
Janitorial No!

Dual swinging doors were in front of him, and he spotted a door on the other side. Plain and grey. So antiseptic. It wasn't going to win any style points.

He scanned the letters GUE.

He stepped through slowly, afraid of what he would find.

Did Blair die before she had time to move?

His beeper vibrated.

I forgot to reset the volume after the classes yesterday!

He turned the sound back on. There was one missed message.

From yesterday at 9:03 am

His first seminar started at 8 am.

He stared at the beeper in his hand. Who had called? He saw the number but didn't recognize it at first.

Duncan looked up and around the room, trying to jog his memory.

The grey door opened while Duncan was still fumbling with his beeper. He came face-to-face with Timothy.

The man standing in front of him didn't resemble his friend at all.

His eyes looked red and swollen, and his hair was disheveled. Timothy hadn't slept in days.

"I... I" he searched for words, but couldn't string them together. "I..."

"There was nothing else they could do for her," Timothy was obviously in shock. His stoic delivery did not have an ounce of personality in it.

"I... wish..." Duncan was still struggling to talk. His own mother came into his mind. Images of the two of them flashed in his memory.

"I called the hotel yesterday when it happened, but you were at your workshop. Beeped you later. Hoped you would get that at least."

"We had to turn the sound off..." The self-doubt and agony were rising.

He's never failed me, and I am never there for him!

Duncan went right back to being that confused and shattered man of 11 years prior. The emotional tsunami began again.

"Blaaaaaair" These same walls felt agony like this from Sarah years ago.

"Dunc, not Blair. Dunc, Dunc. Not Blair."

Duncan tried to understand. He caught his breath.

"Sissy."

Timmy's daughter.

An invisible hand reached inside Duncan's chest and ripped his heart out. The pull had changed. It was vehement. It pushed him backwards. It pressed him against the wall.

"She began to crash the night I saw you."

Answer the pull at a slight cost to you. Do not answer the pull begets a greater cost to all...

"Maybe, if you had come that day... then, maybe..."

The men fell together. Duncan couldn't stand. His soul ached to be rid of all his pain. All his promise. All his...

"Dunc, don't... don't do this to yourself."

It was too late. Duncan's emotions could not be contained.

If I had come when Timmy asked...

Duncan staggered away, Timmy's voice trailing away. The surrounding footsteps rang heavy in his ears. He squinted at the lights above him. He searched for an escape.

Everything was spinning, and he had no control.

A door opened next to him, and he stumbled in. It was quiet and dark, a welcome relief.

He found himself in the elevator. He couldn't read which button he pushed. If there were a sane thought in his brain, it was nowhere to be found.

Timmy. Hannah. SARAH. How many others have I let down?

He understood what his wife went through when she

exploded at him.

No amount of consoling would pull him out of the well he had fallen into.

Chapter Seventeen

T HE ELEVATOR EXECUTED its job tirelessly for hours on end.

People got in, went to their destination and got off. Sometimes a single person, sometimes a group.

Duncan traveled a vertical mile that day. He froze, stuck to the back wall. He got plenty of looks from everyone getting on.

People kept a safe distance.

His face was blotchy and swollen. He had the look of an incompetent prize fighter that couldn't duck the barrage of punches, and every one landed on its target. He spotted his reflection in the shiny interior of his steel coffin.

Who is that?

On one floor, the doors opened, and everything was silent, except for the soft piano music playing, which set a calm ambience. No one was in the elevator with him, and no one got on.

The door stayed open much longer than he expected. He leaned forward and poked his head out.

In front of him was a waiting room with chairs, an empty nurses' station and a wooden doorway with a small vertical glass window in it.

The words 'Infusion Services' appeared in stencil on the wall next to the door.

The elevator door stayed open, as if pleading for him to exit, so Duncan stepped out, into the waiting room. He shuffled over and sat in a chair nearest the wall and corridor.

I can make a quick escape if I need to.

He sat blankly staring at the white wall in front of him. The music gave him a rope to hold on to. All the antiseptic, healing odors that floated through the air downstairs were gone. Grief pounced over and over in between sobs.

He closed his eyes for a moment. He needed to turn his brain off.

"Are you sick too?" The question jolted him awake. He must have dozed off.

Duncan was still foggy and certainly emotional. He stammered. "There's nothing that can be done..." His voice trailed off.

Am I dreaming?

"They said that to me a year ago... but I'm not sure I believed them," the child said.

Duncan looked at him. He couldn't determine an age, and with no hair, it was hard to tell if this was a girl or a boy. Whoever it was, they were in a wheelchair, leaning forward a bit. They didn't look comfortable at all.

I think this is a boy. Duncan struggled to focus.

His eyes are soo... soo clear... and the color... swirling almost — blue to green to brown...

They sat next to each other. Duncan was still stifling his sobs as best he could, but they were only slowing.

"Do you think we get better when we go to Heaven?"

The child's question took Duncan's breath away. He searched for an answer. His head snapped around, and he focused on the child before him.

It couldn't be that simple. Duncan's mind suddenly

became clear and focused. It was like the wind swept away a mist he didn't know was there.

"If..." Duncan stared at his hands.

Is there more than just what passes through my hands?

"If the time is right, we get better here." Duncan paused and realized...

It's all about presence.

"Sometimes we have to wait until Heaven."

The weight that crushed his chest for so long, the guilt, the fear, the self-pity—it started to lift.

Then... The pull. It was different. It was warm. It was gentle.

It was.

He was emptying himself, one sliver at a time, letting go of the doubt that consumed him inside. Something else was filling that void. He realized that whatever had been eating at him vanished—maybe not in a grand, visible way, but in the quietest, most profound way.

He looked down at his arm. A hand rested on Duncan's forearm. Duncan's hand sat on top of his.

Both glowed faintly. There was no mistaking it.

Did he... Was I...

He immediately eyed the floor. He thought he'd find an answer in the tiles.

Something happened.

But his mind was quiet. Gone were the doubts, the sorrow and the pain.

They heard the sound of a door opening and closing... heels clicking on the hard floor. They both spied the same pair of white shoes.

A hand reached out and unlocked the brake on the wheelchair. The nurse smiled gently at the child and spoke his name.

"Come on, DA, it's time for your treatment."

As she took him into the treatment room, DA turned back towards Duncan. He smiled meekly.

Duncan swore he mouthed, *"You're fine"* but no words passed between them.

He sat in the waiting room, and the world slowed around him. The piano music played above him. He inspected the ceiling, but he couldn't find where the speakers were.

Inside him, he could hear a peace that he had never experienced before, but it was a silence that deafened him to everything else.

Duncan rose, holding on to the wall for support.

He wasn't sure if he was even breathing.

He closed his eyes and filled his lungs and held the deep breath in.

He exhaled slowly, opened his eyes, and took a step towards the elevator.

———————◆○◆———————

Chapter Eighteen

D UNCAN WALKED DOWN the hallway in the
Assisted Living center.

McKenna had been there for about a year, several years
after Sissy's passing. He paused for a moment in the
corridor. He leaned his head back to rest against the wall
and closed his eyes.

The sounds in the corridor faded away as he let his
mind drift...

Sissy had been laid to rest in Anderson's Acre.

He attended the service but stayed a reasonable
distance away from everybody, so he wouldn't draw any
attention to himself. Timmy spotted him, placed his
hand over his heart and nodded to Duncan.

That was the last time they had any interaction.

From his spot away from the crowd, there were a few
familiar faces. There were even more he didn't recognize.
Hannah was there with Jacob. He'd sprouted into his

own over the years. Duncan looked on as they went to Timmy and Ronnie, exchanged hugs and walked away.

If they noticed him, they didn't give any indication.

He waited for the group to disperse. Duncan silently went by himself to pay his respects to everyone resting in that sacred and hallowed ground.

Donald.
Carla.
Sissy.
This is where my heart will always be, no matter where this takes me.

He turned and decided to take a drive through the old neighborhood to see if any changes had occurred.

The houses and duplexes were different colors, and none of the scents he could remember were present. He passed the Day Care Center, which was now a clubhouse with a pool.

It hadn't been opened for a while. He circled it a couple of times.

The seesaws are gone. Good riddance.

As he came around, he recognized the back of Blair's house and the neatly lined-up townhouses. A few doors down sat his old home. He pulled over to park to get a better vantage point to look around.

The first townhome was Hannah's. A moving truck sat in the driveway.

Jacob emerged carrying boxes, then returned inside for more. Now in dungarees and a T-shirt, he labored with moving boxes. Hannah had changed into work clothes as well, working inside the truck.

A car pulled up. He couldn't make out a plate, but it was an older beat-up maroon sedan. A woman still dressed for the funeral, got out of the car and walked around the front. That's when he saw her.

SARAH

Hannah came out of the back of the box-truck and paused for a second.

Is she being cautious?

Sarah took a single step towards her, then stopped. Her hands came up to cover her face as Hannah jumped off the back and ran to embrace her.

Duncan couldn't hear the words, but he observed the body language.

They were catching up. Jacob came out with more boxes, and Sarah lifted her hand to show how she remembered him as much smaller. His crate had a bunch of plants, and he pulled one out and then pointed off in the distance.

After a minute, he placed the box in the back of the truck. He reached down into the flower bed, plucked a Daffodil, and handed it to Sarah.

She brought it to her nose and inhaled. Her head drooped for a moment, remembering the first flower he had given to her years ago, but she lifted it back up when Jacob kissed her on the cheek. He went back inside, brought out glasses of water, and then checked on his mother to see if she was okay. She nodded, then he disappeared down the bulkhead.

Their heads bobbed back and forth, affirmative, negative and some shrugs. He picked up a few laughs between them.

Hannah stopped swaying and put her hand on Sarah's arm.

Sarah paused, and for a minute, it seemed like the direction of their conversation had changed. Hannah's hand stayed on Sarah's arm until she finally nodded in agreement. Sarah sat on the rear edge of the moving truck.

Hannah's back was now to Duncan, so that he couldn't make out anything. He could watch only from a distance.

It appeared that Hannah was talking and being very

deliberate. Sarah, guarded at first, looked and winced. Hannah stepped closer, and Sarah leaned in. She reeled back in shock, covering her mouth in a silent gasp.

Hannah turned towards where Duncan sat in his car, but her hands were over her face. From where he was, it appeared clear as day.

A flesh-colored tank top under her open blouse.

She turned back towards Sarah to see her face buried in her hands, weeping. Hannah wrapped her arms around her friend and let her cry. Duncan grimaced at the pain. He could feel it, but the pull did not call to him.

Sarah grasped the truth now.

D uncan opened his eyes. The sounds of the Hospice came back to his ears.

His sight was a little blurry, so he rubbed his hands over his face to clear it up. His head caught up in short order.

He glanced up from where he was leaning. Nurses were passing him by; most of them recognized him because of his more frequent visits. He wandered down the hallway to the center, near the nurses' station. They moved her here a couple of weeks ago, so they would be closer, if needed.

Duncan read the room number, Room 147.

He stepped through the door into another world.

Sterile.
Bland.
Colorless.

There were knick-knacks around the room, but they added little color.

A few cards sat on the windowsill. It was a pretty big window, and the view was very tranquil.

I guess they should have something peaceful to look at.

A frail voice crackled in the air.

"Timmy and Ronnie came by yesterday, brought me that lovely plant." She had a little strength to point at it. It came from Blair, all the way from Hawaii—a potted Yellow Hibiscus.

It was the only real vibrance in the room. Duncan moved over and looked closely. He hadn't seen either of them since the cemetery.

His eyes wandered up to the nurse's whiteboard in the room. In big block printing was the name DRUMMOND, MCKENNA.

Under her name, in black marker, were the letters:

DNR

Duncan ached when he saw it. He turned back to his mother. She appeared so frail.

She was grey now, and her luxurious skin was pale and sunken. Her freckles, once soft and glowing, had been erased by age spots years ago.

Her hands were bony and crooked with arthritis. She had glasses on, and an oxygen feed passed up over her ears, down to her nostrils. More and more machines filled the room over the past weeks, all there to show she was still present.

"I can remember back to when I had just a midwife and a washbasin. Back when I had you." She smiled weakly.

"They all told me…" She coughed a little, then continued, "…that having you was dangerous. That it would end badly for you…" A heavy pause filled the room. "…or for me."

She gained strength in telling the story.

Good for you, girl. You tell 'em.

Duncan knew his mother was as fierce as they come.

She never backed down from a fight, and she never lost either.

None were left to say otherwise.

"Yer faather never left m'side at the end. Y'were born without any effort or pain."

The memory warmed her like a Highland wool sweater.

"Yer faather calmed me and you... You cleansed me, more than you could ever knoow... and f'that, I know I've been blessed more than I d'serve."

"It's not for me to be given any more than I was on that daay." She pulled the light blanket up to her chin.

"Yer faather cared for us all these years, silently. He bore tragedy I'cn'nt put into words." Her gaze wandered to look out the window, as if something was calling to her.

She shifted her weight to reach for a worn scrap on the tray table near the bed.

"Duncan Graham, you take this."

Trembling hands held out the card. It bore a weathered wax seal, a single slice across it. Duncan recognized the faded Graham mark.

She regarded it with love and care, her eyes welled and her lip trembled. This was a look that Duncan had never seen before.

Her delicate features echoed her deep, unspoken personal feelings. She had a look both of longing and of realizing her journey was over.

"It's... where your father lies." McKenna sighed deeply and closed her eyes.

"When it's my time..." she mustered up the strength to prop herself up momentarily, one last act of defiance.

"You WILL lay me next to him," she locked eyes with Duncan.

She slipped back onto the bed.

Her eyelids closed. A wry smile came to her face. She knew she would finally join Ethan and start a new journey at his side.

Her face softened.

The door was open; all she had to do was step through.

Her eyes fluttered open briefly. They were already in

another realm. She turned her head towards her son.

"He gaave you to me, and he never stopped loving us. I've neever stopped loving him."

McKenna reached for Duncan's hand. Trembling, she brought it to her lips and kissed it softly.

She brushed her face with his palm.

Turning towards the window... she slowly pushed his hand away and towards the door, and let go.

Duncan sensed what this meant.

The pull called him away. Gently.

He turned slowly and walked towards the door. He looked back briefly, and her head turned towards the window.

He turned away, took a step through the door and paused.

He closed his eyes... and he heard the blip of her heart monitor slow...   ... then, stop.

For a moment, he felt it. The hoof falls of a horse.

Chapter Nineteen

A NURSE WHEELED an empty gurney past a Physical Therapy room.

The wheels made an awful racket that bounced off the walls. The hallway was pretty busy at times, but when it was barren, you could hear almost everything happening there.

Foot scrape / Click
Foot scrape / Click

Someone with a cane.

Stomp / Squeaky wheel
Stomp / Squeaky wheel

Someone on one of those knee scooter things.

Whiiiiz Whiiiiz Whiiiiz Whiiiiz

Wheelchair. Definitely a wheelchair.

DA was fantastic at guessing the sounds of things

coming down the halls. He excelled at singling out the noises in the PT facility, too.

Plop plop plop plop

Someone bouncing a weighted ball against a small kickback trampoline.

RrrrrRrrrrRrrrrRrrrrRrrrr for 10 minutes straight

Somebody's on the bike. For sure on the bike.

"Okay, DA, time to go back to your room." The transport facilitator helped him into the wheelchair.

You know I can do this.

"I know what you're thinking. Yes, you can probably do this... but rules are rules."

"Until you walk out that door, you get a ride when you leave a PT appointment."

The TF was not having any funny business.

They rode the 'moving sardine can' to the 4th floor, Rehab and Recovery wing. He hated the elevator. The music was almost as bad as the Physical Therapy. They traveled up to their floor, where the doors opened. DA grabbed the wheels and rolled himself off the elevator.

I told you I could do it myself.

The TF smiled to himself. It was funny how DA *always* got away from him. Mrs. Stallings was waiting.

"There you are, young man! I was thinking you were never coming back up!"

Jamie Marshall-Stallings had been with the Hospital for almost 5 years and had accumulated every award possible. They even made up a few. Whatever they made up? Didn't matter.

She earned it. She had a depth of empathy that inspired those around her to improve themselves.

The TF gave DA a high-five and disappeared back down the elevator.

You could hear the beeps and whoosh of oxygen, the soft bells for Nurse calls to rooms; it was way different up here than down at PT.

Physical Therapy was a struggle for most people. They would concentrate a lot and not say much. Up here, it was a bustle, because people were either out of long-term treatment or because they were in for a brief stay.

DA liked the slow roll that Mrs. Stallings took down the hall. He was in no rush, and he got to say hi to the staff as he passed by.

Mrs. Stallings stopped as if she had hit a wall. She was looking at DA's chart.

"You did 30 squats today? 30??? Do you know what that means?"

She rushed DA over to the large central Nurse's station in the middle of the floor. Over the station hung a bell. She grabbed the long rope attached to the ringer and handed it to DA.

"Ring IT!" she implored.

The joy on her face gave DA the strength to pull that much harder.

RINGRINGRINGRINGRINGRINGRING

The sound traveled down the halls, and cheers rose from all the different rooms.

"DA'S GOING HOME!!!!"

You couldn't hide his beaming smile.

Every nurse on the floor came over to congratulate him. This absolutely made their career's worth it.

They all viewed his struggle. They all studied his pain.

They all watched as he overcame the odds.

They ALL got to see him leave.

ALIVE.

DA was the center of attention as all the nurses came by to congratulate the boy they had been tending to over the years. DA didn't mind the attention one bit.

Mrs. Stallings finally shooed all the nurses back to the nursing station. It was almost shift change, with dinner coming up soon.

DA slumped a little, the smile still on his face. It had been a long day for him.

"Tired, Champ? Let's get you back to your room so you can have some food, then rest."

The floor was almost silent now.

Down at this end, it's much quieter. I hate it.

As they moved down the hall, they passed Room 406. Harsh, thick coughing echoed from within. DA grabbed the wheels on his chair to stop.

Something had guided his hands to the wheels.

"What's up, buddy?" she asked.

He was peering into the room. All he made out were tiny feet under a blanket. There were more coughs, and they jolted with each one.

They were raspy, and you could tell that it wasn't a good cough. They were heavy and from deep inside a small chest.

Mrs. Stallings' eyes peered over the boy in the wheelchair.

I was that age once, when Dunc... thought Jamie.

"I'm going in." DA didn't even ask permission.

He stood slowly, as if *something was helping him stand.* Jamie held the wheelchair steady. His legs were wobbly, and he steadied himself on the arms.

Jamie glanced back at the nurses' station, where several were silently watching.

Her hand came off the handle of the chair for a moment, waving them over to watch. They gathered quietly, keeping their distance.

DA took a step. He paused to be sure he was stable.

Answer the pull when it bids you to follow...

He took another. He grabbed the wall to stay upright.

Into the room he stepped.
The hallway melted away. Walls, doors, and lights all vanished. The sights and sounds all disappeared.

J amie Marshall-Stallings stood alone, watching. Her voice carried over the scene like a prayer.

Daniel Abbott went into that room that day and gave hope to a sick child.

For the next 56 years, Daniel Abbott went into the rooms of thousands of sick children and gave them all the same courage.

He became and thrived as the Hospital's Ambassador of Hope.

DA wheeled out every child that got to go home, just like he had done all those years ago.

He celebrated with them when they had joy and watched as they squeezed into a car and drove off with their family.

He ministered to the families in need when they didn't get to go home.

He worked with me for the rest of my career, visited often when I retired and gave the sermon at my funeral.

DA passed, surrounded by family and friends, at the age of 72.

The hospital later renamed the recovery wing.

It is now called the Daniel Abbott Wing of Hope—a tribute to the man who touched so many lives.

A plaque hangs at the front of the Hospital in remembrance.

Chapter Twenty

I T WAS A DREARY DAY in Crieff, Scotland.

The buildings were ancient and utilitarian. They served their purpose and nothing more. It was a long cry from the vibe of the big city.

Heritage ran deep here.

The foundations of every building, constructed on the backs of their Heritage.

The food? The way they toiled the land? The way they played when they could play? The way they worshiped?

Heritage.

That, which burned in their very soul. Every villager knew it. Had It. Clung to it like dew on the early morning meadow grass.

At one end of the village, a fairground that dated back decades. At the other? A cemetery that dated back quite a bit further.

One end celebrated life and the future. The other end celebrated life and the past.

Beyond the hallowed ground was the River Earn. It was the pillar that brought life and tragedy together, over and over.

It just was. Never-ending and never stopping. The witness to events in time, but never revealed.

In the cemetery were two locals. It had only a Caretaker, but no official workers.

They took care of their own. Unflappable. Unquestioning.

Heritage.

In a plot, they toiled away at the task at hand.

The first, digging at the ground,

"It's a dreich day"
Dismal indeed.

"'Tis true, lad. But the grey matches the mood of the daay."

"Aye. A saad day to be sure."

"Buut finally, The Provost is crouss, after all these

years."
Happy, finally.

"What a place to coorie Mother McKenna, finally,
w'it her man."
Together.

"Whit's fur ye'll no go by ye! The Provost gets his final
wish."
It was meant to happen.

"Dinnae think it would happen. Graham and
Drummond, Hell mend ye! To finally close t'ha Clan
divide."

"Ah dinnae ken, goes back a long way lad."
It does go back a long way; how could you not know?

A long pause passed between them.

After leaning on the shovels for a minute, the first
worker spoke slowly.

"Aye, but Bonnie Mother McKenna's come home to
her Valley."

Hours south, a different world was presenting itself
to an unknown visitor.

Duncan peered out the car window.

The Caretaker of the Cemetery sent a car to pick him up. The other transport arrangements had already been made.

Duncan said he would get a rental and drive, but the caretaker insisted. "Better to relax after such a long trip," the caretaker said.

"I'll be prepared to receive you at 3 pm. My man can give you a bit of history on the waay here. 'Tis a wee bit from Edinburgh, and there is much to see and learn."

So, after exchanging arrival times and the details for McKenna's final cortege, they hung up the phone.

Heritage had rules yet unknown to Duncan.

He would ride in a separate vehicle.

McKenna would take the final coffin road alone.

It'll be a long flight. He is probably right. Maybe I'll nap on the way.

They drove away from the airport and headed out.

Rolling hills and lush pastures full of livestock, zoomed past the windows. Mountains could be seen in the distance, their dark grey contrasting against the cloudy light grey sky.

Everything was a shade of grey. Everything. " 'Til clear uup a bit faarther north," the caretaker's man said.

"What do I call you?" Duncan's curiosity finally got the better of him.

"You can call me Boyd," he answered back with a substantial tone.

"The Crieff caretaker told me you were a maan of import, so you'll forgive me if I call you Sir. Allow me thaat?"

The road was long and winding. Every once in a while, you'd spy a village in the offing. Or at least a steeple would show there might be a village there. After almost an hour of silence, Boyd finally spoke.

"We are coming uup to what, in the paast, be known as Lochlane."

Duncan viewed the mountains in front of them as they got closer. To the left, grasslands as far as he surveyed and hills in the distance.

"This 'ere on the right is the River Earn. Lifeblood of this whole area."

"That 'amlet off in the distance? That is Crieff. Used to be all called Lochlane, but o'er the years, things 'ave a way of changing, eh Lad?"

"That they do."

They sure do.

Change was Duncan's home address. He glimpsed his face in the rear-view mirror. His hair was longer, and his face spoke of a missing razor.

The vehicle slowed.

"See, I told you. Clear up nort' ," The sun was poking through the clouds.

The car waited to turn left. The driver turned around to look at Duncan.

"Dunna you worry, we git you a proper shower when we arrive at the village."

Boyd pulled off into a lot next to a building.

Boyd pointed to the left. "Crieff Visitor Center. Best plaace to find local facts, trinkets, history, and get a lay of the land 'ere." He got out of the car, came back and opened the door for Duncan.

He stepped out and stretched his legs. He didn't realize he had been sitting for so long.

"We's still got a little to goo, but good to stretch now and not fall flat on yer faace in frunt of everybody. No, sir, not good t'all."

Duncan surveyed his surroundings. He had memories of this place.

Were they real or ones he dreamt about?

To his left, above a small building, were the words. *PLANT CENTER.*

On a small set of shelves out in front, he spotted them.

Alocasia. Elephant ear plants. He hadn't seen one since Sa....

Boyd stepped in front of him. He raised his hand to the right.

"Drummond Clan land, used to be." He pointed off to the left, "Graham Clan land."

"It's all changed now. Baird's Monument, named after General Sir D Baird, is in the distance, paart of this is King George's Field. Down'ere to the right, the clans stopped fighting and staarted 'aving competition. Skin on skin. Best man on best man. That's 'ow the fighting finally stopped."

Duncan recalled his mother telling him stories of the clans and the clashes. And here was the very ground she spoke of. He focused on the terra under his shoes.

How many others have walked here?

Duncan marveled at how real it was.

"That tradition continues today at the Crieff Highland Gathering, o'er on the Fairgrounds."

Duncan found himself wandering up the road and onto the bridge. Boyd came up beside him.

"This..." He pointed straight ahead, to where the river splits in two, one branch west, one branch east, "...this is McKenna's Valley."

"We call it McKenna's Glen. You'll not find it on any maps, but we know where t'is."

Duncan's eyes welled up. A heritage he never understood reached out from beyond and took hold of him.

Boyd noticed Duncan drying his eyes with a kerchief.

"Aye, sir. I din'nah mean to shake you so."

"I've never heard my mother's name used like that."

Her quiet reserve and peacefulness all lay out on the gentle, lush grasses before him.

Her name. This meadow. The beauty of the landscape tied to the beauty of his mother was not lost on him.

"Lad, pray, McKenna? McKenna Drummond, be your mu'um?"

Duncan bowed his head and answered in a whisper.

"She is."

"You be…" Boyd couldn't get the words out.

"Duncan."

Boyd stumbled back. "I… I.. Din'nah know." I beg for.. for..giveness."

Boyd's reaction took him by surprise.

"You know of me?"

The caretaker's man regarded him for a moment with his jaw clenched, stifling back tears.

"Aye. The whole of the valley knows of you."

They stood for a minute. Boyd's posture changed in an instant. His shoulders pulled back, jaw clenched. He changed from tour guide to Sentinel in the space of a breath.

His cool green eyes struggled to contain his tears.

Boyd finally peeked at his watch.

"It's 2:30. We have got to go, Sir."

He started back towards the car, sending a text message as he walked.

"Slow down!" Duncan fell behind, but made ground up quickly. Boyd swung his door open and let him slide in. He got in front, started the car and proceeded over the bridge. He didn't say another word.

B oyd came upon a small road with a roundabout on it—a tall gate with an opening big enough for a car, and one to the side for pedestrians.

He parked outside the gate.

"Y'dn'nt paark on the Sacred Ground inside th' gate." Boyd finally said, educating Duncan on more mysteries of the Valley. They opened the heavy gate and stepped through.

On the other side of the gate, they regarded the peacefulness of the Valley laid out before them.

"It's like a postcard from Heaven," Duncan whispered to himself.

They took a few steps, and inside the Crieff Cemetery

entrance was a marker, worn and weathered by the passage of time and the events of the region. History had almost wiped it from existence.

They passed the stone slowly. As Boyd passed, he pressed his lips to the crucifix around his neck.

"Everyone in the Valley wears one; it hangs o'er our hearts."

Duncan paused and glanced at the stone.

You could discern only the remaining letters carved deep into the cemetery fieldstone.

D G L

What is this place I am drawn to and know nothing about?

Duncan couldn't take his eyes off the marker. Boyd waited off to the side and looked on while the past called to Duncan.

"An ancient relic, that is. I aam not surpriised you are draawn to it."

"That be the sacred resting place of Dugald."

"Dugald Graham." The name escaped from Duncan's lips.

A name he had not spoken in decades, but was marked forever in his memory.

Duncan looked at his hands, and his eyes shot up to meet Boyd's.

Could this be the source of it? The pull???

"Aaftar me, Sir." Boyd brought his attention back to the moment at hand. The men walked down the path, and several family marker areas surrounded them. Duncan's head was on a swivel. There was so much to take in.

It wound down, and Duncan could see one plot directly in front of him. It sat apart from the others, clearly in a place of honor.

Boyd stopped and let him approach on his own.

I'll not go any further until he asks me to.

Boyd was on hallowed ground.

There before Duncan was a massive stone that was two plots wide.

It was a majestic granite marker, dwarfing the others around it.

'GRAHAM' etched deep in bold letters across the top, and a Celtic Cross carved in the middle.

To Duncan's right, the name 'Ethan'.

Above Ethan's name appeared, also carved, 'PROVOST' with his birth and death dates below.

On Duncan's left, at Ethan's right hand, was a stark contrast. A simple shrouded female carving from the shoulders up and the Drummond Standard.

Her name, 'McKenna', appeared below, followed only by her birth year.

The open grave lay ready, and flowers covered the area. Her casket was already there, waiting.

He didn't try to stop the tears. She was finally going to be home.

The massive marker had a spot on it that revealed a worn, smooth edge near the corner on Ethan's side of the monument.

"People still come till this daay to lay hands on his stone," Boyd said with a hushed reverence.

Duncan took a handkerchief to dry his eyes. He carefully put it back in his pocket. He scanned to his left, and something caught his eye.

Another smaller engraved headstone read...

Duncan
Sarah
...with their birth dates below.

Their names united by a carved ivy vine... He stared in disbelief.

How would... did he know?

Duncan didn't panic. He didn't question. He accepted that he was where fate led him. The land his father, Ethan, bled into many years ago was reaching out to his progeny.

A voice came from behind, but he didn't turn.

"3 pm. I told you I'd be ready to receive you, so here I am, Boy." The Caretaker had an old, leathery voice.

Duncan turned around, his face still lowered. He drew a breath, straightened his back and lifted his head.

He came face-to-face with dozens of people. Drummond and Graham Tartans were everywhere.

The gravediggers were there, dressed in opposing clan kilts.

The ages ranged from small children to older, hardened villagers.

An elder, clad in the full regalia of the Drummond

tartan with a decorated kilt, stood in front of him. His face traced the wisdom of his years. He stepped forward to regard Duncan.

"McKenna," he said, his voice husky with emotion, "was a woman of strength and spirit."

"Blessed was I to call her sister... and I have missed her, these many years."

Too many years.

He drew a breath. "And your faather, the Provost... he loved her with a passion that could mend old wounds."

"As a child, I stood witness to the day your Faather joined our clans with his act of bravery and loyalty for Lady McKenna."

A long pause followed as Duncan surveyed his surroundings, with his mouth open in disbelief.

He had knowledge of my Father?
My Mother's brother?
My kin???

His mind raced, and it made his knees weak.

"You've come before this resting place, but look back upon the path, towards the left of the gate."

The crowd turned as one.

"See yon chapel hidden within the trees? Built by Drummond and Graham clans with Drummond and Graham stone." The elder took a deep breath.

"That, m'boy, McKenna Chapel."

"The children of this village? All Baptised in that chapel. Y'not find a more Revered woman in this valley."

Heads bowed as one to pray silently.

The Elder's duty weighed upon him as he continued, "Your faaather built it next to Dugald Albios."

Every person pressed their crucifix to their lips and then secreted away their artifacts of faith.

Close to their hearts... Duncan witnessed dozens of acts of faith.

"They both watch over and protect this place of rest."

The Elder bowed his head, withdrew his crucifix from under his sweater, and kissed it with centuries of faith behind the gesture.

As Fergus had generations prior. In the presence of Dugald, in the House of Kieran Drummond, to save a lad marked by a Clan name by no fault of his own.

Gently, he placed it back in his sweater and

straightened himself to stand tall in front of Duncan. He seemed to be renewed, present and purposeful.

He paused, his piercing gaze settling on Duncan.

He stepped forward and whispered in a hushed and reverent tone. Their agency was private between them.

"Laddy, here in the sight of God and all present,"

A deep breath filled his lungs.

"D'ye have the Gift of the Hands? Like yer faather did?"

Duncan had noticed his crooked and arthritic hands when he handled his crucifix.

Duncan's heart was replete with pride, empathy and a sense of belonging.

He took the Elder's hands and peered directly into his soul... but didn't say a word.

The Elder's eyes welled up with tears. One rolled down his cheek. This moment was for them, private, intense—*and personal.*

The warmth witnessed only by them. The light shone for them, alone.

Duncan gently let go of the elder's hand, stroked

his face, and looked towards those gathered. The Elder looked down at his hand, wounded and crippled in defense of Ethan, so many years ago.

Healed by the very man The Provost held in such high esteem. He looked up at Duncan as the crowd surrounded him...

Duncan stepped away from the elder. A voice jabbed at the air. "Let me pass."

The crowd parted.

Alan Drummond?

Alan stepped forward. The son of the Elder, he stopped in front of Duncan. He was wearing both tartans—Drummond and Graham—woven with purpose, not fashion.

Alan recounted with reverence, "My faather bade me go to you... and protect you."

His eyes met Duncan's. They both stared at the Elder.

"I swore to him I'd guard the Legacy to my very core. If it required my life, it only need ask."

With that, he took Duncan's hand and kissed it, bowed his head and moved to take his place at his Father's side.

Alan's memories rushed back:

FLASH

He was at Sissy's funeral, mixed in with the crowd, but unseen. Duncan never got close enough to see him.

FLASH

He was at some of Jacob's games, in the stands. He went to the boosters' tables and made donations in Duncan's name. Duncan hung around the fence by the dugout; Alan sat blended with the crowd, at a safe distance.

FLASH

He brought McKenna news the day of her beloved's murder, nay, sacrifice at the hands of dark forces trying to keep to the old ways. He gave her the Interment Notice bearing the Sliced Graham seal, so that she may join him in death.

FLASH

Alan helped devise surprises with Timmy and made sure he understood what was being planned. They didn't want Duncan to bear worry about any of it.

FLASH

McKenna and Alan talked about what Alan's father, her brother, had charged him to do, and she begged Alan to do the same. He brought McKenna letters from Ethan. Letters from the Homeland, and reported back about Ethan's unseen lineage.

FLASH

Alan had been watching Duncan the night he disappeared. He saw exactly where he was the whole time. Alan called McKenna, and she drove out to meet him. They came in together. Duncan never spotted Alan's car in the parking lot.

FLASH

Alan heard there was a blowup between Sarah and Hannah. He parked across the street from Duncan's house after he learned about it. He waited outside until Duncan came home. He could hear the arguing. He burst in when he did to try to de-escalate. He took Sarah away to protect Duncan from further damage.

Alan had joined his Father at his right hand.
The two cemetery workers joined them.
The Caretaker stepped alongside Duncan.

"We have one task to complete, to make them whole," the Caretaker whispered to Duncan.

"Watch the others and do as they do."

They stepped to McKenna's casket.

Three straps were laid out on each side, and each took a spot.

They wrapped the straps over their shoulders, around the back of their necks and gripped the excess with their opposite hands.

"Alright, Lads. Gentle, that."

They lowered McKenna to her rightful place.

The River Earn nearby, bore witness, yet again.

Chapter
Twenty-One

D UNCAN STAYED IN Crieff for three months.

Alan served as his guide, providing details about how Ethan would talk of his mother as being his saving angel. He had never intended to unite the clans, but his love and compassion for McKenna did just that.

She became lore through Ethan's words.

The two clans joined him to build the chapel. It took 5 years to build.

Everything had a purpose. You either served the land, or you served each other.

"Even when you have nothing left to your name, you can still serve." That is what Ethan taught.

"When Finlay sent me to you, you spoke the same testament. I needn't hear more." He drew a deep breath. "I shared it with your mother that you were her Ethan, in a different person."

"I shared it with Ethan himself in letters I wrote home. Ethan knew you for the calling, and he spoke the truth."

Finlay shared stories of how Ethan won everyone over. Every time he told a story, Ethan was a little taller, or the horse was bigger. When Ethan brandished his sword? It was either brightly polished or the sun reflected off it just right.

Once, Duncan thought Finlay said lightning came from it.

Finlay promised to share the story of Ethan's sacrifice on the very steps of McKenna's Chapel, at the right time.

This was not the right time for such a testament.

Alan took Duncan around the town. Word had already spread that McKenna's boy was in Crieff. Strangers came up to him to pay their respects. Everyone he met knew of his mother. People openly wept when embracing Duncan.

Duncan came to realize she had been a living legend to those still within Crieff.

Wandering the town on a bright and sunny day, Alan and Duncan went to the Crieff and Strathearn Museum. Duncan studied the displays and artifacts. They pulled him across decades and centuries of history. The Graham name appeared often, as did the Drummond name.

Everywhere he went, everyone wanted a minute with McKenna's son. Once the minute passed, they left him in peace.

Alan had warned Duncan that he would draw a lot of attention... but he never imagined it would be this much.

BOOOM
What was that?
BOOOM
BOOOM

"The cannons have sounded thrice! Come lad, you'll see what yer Faather had wrought!"

Alan and Duncan sprinted up the lane. The street lights were decorated in all manner of colors. The scent of open-fire cooking invaded his nostrils. Music filled the air, and on top of it, a cheering crowd roared with pleasure.

"This be the Highland Games. This is what replaced our Clan hatred, my cousin. Indeed, Belenos has brought you home!"

For hours, dance, celebration and a joy for life swaddled Duncan in ways he had never experienced. Powerful men battled in various areas of the field. Drummond and Graham kilts dazzled your eyes as far as you could observe.

No one died. No one hated. Competitors squared off, and then both would rejoice after the battle.

TOGETHER.

Best Man against Best Man.

Duncan and Alan stopped in front of one such competition.

"This be known as 'Clach cuid fir'."

"Leefting stoones. Taake it from the groound. Set it upon your laap, then leeft it to the plaatform. Test of streength." Alan explained with pride.

They watched as man after man started with a small stone and worked his way to larger stones. When a man could lift no more, he withdrew... and received praise from all his competitors.

A voice came over the loudspeaker mounted on the pole.

"Bothan Dinnie!"

The crowd erupted. Clearly, he was well-loved at the games. "Related to the great Dinnie name. Famous, 'e is." Alan provided a running commentary.

Bothan, clad in a black kilt with a single red sash, lumbered to the first stone.

He cut an intimidating figure.

The competitors cheered him on.

This was a one-man fight, but the entire field filled and energized him.

He beat upon his chest, first the left side and then the right.

His breath came in spurts, and he prepared to battle the stone incarnate.

A horn sounded, and he was off. The competitors egged him on. The crowd, dizzy with excitement.

One Stone.

Two.

Three. Four. Five.

Six.

He reached the seventh stone. He labored to get it in his lap.

No man had reached the seventh stone in this competition. Frenzy surrounded him.

Alan and Duncan cheered him on, just feet from him, behind a small wall.

Bothan leaned back and hefted the stone to his chest.

He panted under the effort. All he needed to do was move forward two paces and place it on the platform.

One step. He steadied himself.

Second step. He roared with effort.

The stone sat at the edge of the barrel platform.

The crowd was whipped into bedlam.

In slow motion, the stone slipped from his grip.

Bothan jumped to clear the falling stone.

But not fast enough. It landed on his left shin and foot. It crushed the bone and ankle.

The stone rolled off, but you could see the devastating injury.

Duncan didn't hesitate. He bounded over the wall directly to Bothan.

He didn't need the pull. He knew what he must do.

He kneeled and placed his hand over Bothan's eyes, then moved to his leg.

The warmth IGNITED but did not burn.

The light RADIATED but did not blind.

"GET UP. FIGHT ANOTHER DAY. YOU'RE FINE."

The field was silent.

Bothan stood tall before Duncan. He reached down with one arm and helped Duncan to his feet.

The eyes of the two men locked upon each other. Duncan placed his hand over the heart of the warrior.

Bothan dropped to one knee and lowered his head in piety. Duncan's eyes cascaded over the hushed crowd.

A person in the stands was heard to say, "That... th... that was Lady McKenna's boy..."

Crucifixes being kissed appeared all over the grounds.

The legacy had returned to Crieff. And everyone saw it.

Duncan had his peace. He had joy in his life.

More importantly, he had family he could count on.

Crieff embraced him without question, judgement or expectation.

Duncan was sorry to leave, but he promised to journey back to his roots. He had so much more to learn, and took his oath to return.

He wanted to clean up some loose ends, and Crieff sensed his calling to lie elsewhere.

B oyd insisted on driving him back to the airport. They stopped at the family plot.

Duncan smiled.

His mother was where she wanted to be.

He stopped at her Chapel.

It was simple, had roughly hewn pews, and an Altar

built by reverent hands paying homage to a woman present in deeds and actions only.

A pair of crossed swords was the only decoration on the inside of the wall, above an inscription chiseled into the stone, "Wins Awa"

One sword was etched with the letters LD. The second marked by FD, upon the hilt.

A young family was celebrating a baptism. They invited him to pour the Holy Water. He let the Clergyman do the job he was there to do, but bestowed all his wishes and prayers on them as he exited with a grace that could only come from this sacred place.

Boyd talked his ear off on the way back to the airport, and Duncan sat in the front seat. He wasn't a man of import. He was just a man.

Once at the airport, the car sat in the drop-off area for a few moments.

Neither man knew what to say.

Duncan opened the car door; Boyd jumped out and grabbed his bag from the back seat. He dropped the suitcase at Duncan's feet and stood tall. Duncan pondered the bag in front of his shoes.

Next time, I won't need a bag.

He wished Boyd well and hoped to see him again soon.

Boyd reached to his jacket lapel and pulled off his Graham Lapel Badge Pin. He placed it on Duncan's lapel, leaned forward and kissed it with solemnity.

"Come back to us soon, lad."

Boyd wheeled and walked back to the car, nodded slightly, climbed back in, and drove off.

Duncan turned and went into the terminal.

Once boarded on his flight, he pulled a journal from his bag. He had written so much over the course of his trip to Crieff. He wanted to read during the entire flight, but sleep settled into his bones.

His flight was uneventful. He woke up just as they landed.

B ag slung over his shoulder, he headed straight for the Taxi Stand. He hailed a cab, got in and headed to the school he used to teach at. He wanted to say goodbye to the staff. He came into the office, and almost nobody knew him. His hair was pretty scruffy, and he now had a full three-month beard.

But the Superintendent happened to be there and recognized his voice. It was full of life and light, a stark contrast to how serious he was in the past.

He spoke to the Superintendent for a minute and relayed that he was going to travel to see where life brought him. The Superintendent understood. He had been one of the ones in the Hall many years ago.

This man possessed the same drive as before, but this time, he had control of what was happening in his world. They shook hands, and Duncan spun and walked out.

Down the street he went, then turned the corner two blocks down. The medical center was straight up this road about half a mile. He started for it. A block down, he passed a storefront, a little run-down, and quite a few people were milling about outside.

He stopped and got a good look at his reflection in the window. He needed a haircut and a shave. Probably a good sandblasting, too.

He focused on the words on the glass.

Brown's Soup Kitchen.

He studied many faces as he stood in line. Looking past the people, he could see the meager counter staff.

He felt drawn to enter.

He walked inside and halted for a moment. There was a palpable somberness in the room. Someone handed him a tray and pointed him to the line to the right.

"Oh no, I'm here to help. It looks like you need some."

"Mr. Brown. Mr. Brown!" A man came out of the back room.

"This guy says he wants to help. Can you use him?" He looked him over once and said, "Sure, come with me." He crooked a finger for Duncan to follow him.

A SCAR

"*Reggie?*"

"Yeah, who are you?" he answered.

"You don't recognize me? I know I look like crap, but... it's Duncan!"

A look of disbelief came over his face, but slowly the recognition came.

For the next hour, they talked while they served food, gave away groceries, helped people with clothing and gave out coffee. Reggie had received a large tip in his cab one day, and he decided to give back to those in need. That was a few months back, and it grew into a mission in the area. Duncan learned there were missions all around the country and around the world.

They all needed the same thing.

Someone to be present.

Chapter
Twenty-Two

D UNCAN DECIDED after a few months to leave
Reggie's Soup Kitchen.

He had amassed a lot of contacts, and he realized he
needed to be overseas.

He had shaved and gotten a haircut. He cleaned up
nicely. He settled on a mission that let him travel any
path he chose. He had regular stops to contact the home
office.

He learned he could use his hands well enough to ask
questions, without knowing the language of the areas he
visited.

Many villages were poor, but they always fed him. He
met with children and adults alike.

He would solve simple problems like fixing a watering
mechanism or perhaps rebuilding a stone wall. Even
doing some tasks in the field, where he would peel off his
shirt and tan under the sun.

Rocks slipped from his hands when they were wet; his skin chafed when they were dry. Blisters were a passage of strength, not an inconvenience.

The smell of cooking food was never unwelcome.

It was WAY hotter in some of these jungles than at home.

The sweat proved it.

Perspiration was a sign of a job well done. He still didn't burn. He didn't need to show off because there was never anyone to impress. Some of the older villagers could outwork him and not bat an eye.

He roamed into one village and came across a group sitting outside a house. They were using a language he didn't understand.

A young boy was uttering to others present. Duncan felt the boy needed help, but he did not know what was happening. He was drawn to the boy.

He squatted down, and the boy spoke a barrage of sounds that made no sense. Duncan put his hand on the boy's shoulder. He placed his index finger to his lips. The boy understood.

Duncan turned his palms up and shrugged his shoulders as if to ask, "What's up?"

The child pointed to his leg, made a fist, and struck his shin hard. The boy signaled toward the hut. He pulled Duncan in. A woman was tending to a man, who was clearly in pain. She was washing his leg with a dirty cloth. The makeshift water vessel was full of a brackish liquid.

Duncan gathered he was in distress. A wobbly homemade stool creaked under him as he sat. He lifted the wet rag and studied the gash on the man's leg. He soaked the cloth in the water so that he could clean the wound a little.

Everyone filled the hut, speaking, but Duncan couldn't make sense of what they said.

The man appeared to be the Patriarch of this little group.

Duncan surveyed the group quickly, scanning their faces, then looked back to the boy. He put his index finger to his lips, pointed to everyone, and then the door. The boy started pulling people out of the hut.

Alone with the man, Duncan patted his head, then touched his shoulder. His breathing eased. Duncan took one last look around, then closed his eyes.

The warmth came to him immediately. He placed his hands on the man's leg. The light filled the hut.

The brilliance quickly dissipated, and the man was standing before him with a quizzical look on his face.

Duncan tried to stand, but knew he couldn't, but it was a small price to pay. The man scanned his surroundings, grabbed a handle of a field tool, and handed it to him to lean against.

Duncan pulled himself up. He popped the implement on the end off easily, then took several weak steps and left the hut, leaning on the makeshift staff. The group watched in silence until the man came out, when the chatter started again. The group's sound changed.

He heard women crying. He continued down the path slowly, with the makeshift staff to help him. Behind him, he heard someone running, getting closer. He turned to look. It was the boy.

He stared at Duncan.

Duncan smiled, then turned, continuing on his way.

He visited many villages—some in rainforests, some in jungles. There were ones on a mountainside, some next to rivers. Humidity hung like a tapestry in these foreign lands. The desert villages were all different. Some hot, some hotter.

Some were not hot but devoid of water. He walked over mountains, into valleys and along footpaths that had been carved out of time itself. There was never a destination; he went where his feet led him.

Over the months of wandering, he kept the staff for stability. It was his traveling companion now.

As he traveled along, the sound of helicopters became increasingly prevalent. He was drawn to a noise that had no business in this remote area.

He followed the noise to a clearing. A group of people wearing armbands, helping people who were barely clothed. He could see people offering water, and many of them were too weak to drink.

Some were receiving emergency IVs. Familiar languages rang through the air. Some French, maybe Spanish.

English. Not only English, but American English.

He moved through the crowd to a small group huddled over a sickly infant. The infant was on a small tuft of hay, surrounded by a blanket. Staff were gently bathing her, and someone who appeared to be her mother was standing, near her head. Her hands were clasped in both agony and hope.

A person was kneeling above the infant, trying to coax her to take a sip from a baby bottle filled with water. She gently squeezed the bottle, and a couple of drops appeared. She whetted the baby's lips. Almost immediately, the baby puckered to get her lips wet.

She did it again, with the same reaction.

Slowly, she brought the bottle closer, touched her mouth with the nipple, and the baby instinctively took to it and started drinking.

"Come on. Come on," the voice softly beckoned. "Your momma's right there. Come on, open your eyes."

Duncan watched intently, in silence.

He was present.

"That's it. That's it."

"Just do the right thing..."

It hit Duncan like lightning.

"Just do the right thing... that's it, that's IT!"

The baby's eyes fluttered open.

The mother dropped to her knees next to her baby.

The woman leaned back, when Duncan's hand grazed her shoulder.

—Goosebumps shot through her whole body

Her head spun around, and she faced a staff.

A Graham Lapel Badge Pin was affixed to it.

Why would that be...

Memories flashed before her eyes.

Alocasia plants.
Anderson's Acre.
The Pub outside James Bend.
The Hall.

Her eyes shot up as she pulled the head covering off.

SARAH

She took him in for a minute.

He reached out slowly, afraid.

He stroked her cheek.

—Goosebumps

She took his hand in hers, and she gently pressed it to her lips.

Years of an unspoken misunderstanding faded like a mist over an untapped landscape.

She bowed her head on it, held it to her forehead and started to weep.

Chapter Twenty-Three

Epilogue

Lost in the hustle and bustle of the real world, there in Crieff near the River Earn, lies an alleyway.

Countless clansmen have trodden upon its ancient cobblestones.

You have to seek it out—it's not easily found—but if you look hard enough; the path becomes clear.

A street sign clings to the side of a building, as old as it is strong.

It reads: Dugald Wynd.

Here, noise fades into an inward silence. The smells, unfamiliar yet soothing to the bruises of the soul.

The buildings stand resolute—firm in their purpose, protective of their nature.

Leaning against the building is a crooked stick. A patch of worn deerskin flutters, gently guiding you to daunder forth.

A Graham Lapel Badge Pin affixed to the staff, glints in a Sun that never stops shining.

A Griffin Crest Pin attached, just above it.

Separate, yet together.

And if you follow it to the end, there before you stands a pub. A single stone shingle hangs from a beam that looks like it had burned in Hades itself.

The battered door next to it gave silent witness to that battle.

Etched upon that stone shingle, weathered by wind and time, it simply says:

"Let Dugald Albios walk with you...

...on your path."

The Venerated Legacy

More from Mickey Stone

Stone of Alisanos, the second book in **THE VENERATED LEGACY** series, follows the story of Provost *Ethan Graham*. Travel with him as he faces challenges, teachings, love and sacrifice... all to better others, even as it costs him dearly. Love is what drives him; Unification is what he wishes for; corrupt forces are what he must face.

Danu of Talamh, the third book in **THE VENERATED LEGACY** series, tells the Legend of *Dugald Graham*, displaced from his home in Ireland at an early age. He travels, as an orphan, to Scotland and finds the Graham Clan, who cares for and adopts him as one of their own. The kindness shown to him is amplified in mysterious ways when Dugald prays for kindness for ALL men... and he is answered and bestowed a gift that passes across generations.

Sacred or Secret, the fourth book in **THE VENERATED LEGACY** series, follows *Jamie Marshall-Stallings and Daniel Abbott (DA)* on their incredible work at the James Medical Center. *Duncan*

Graham's legacy ripples through those who he comes in contact with. A reporter, *Stella*, comes to James Bend to do a fluff piece on some incredible people at the Medical Center, and finds herself in the middle of something she can't explain, doesn't believe... and is not sure if it should be exposed. ˙

Cloaked Content, the fifth book in **THE VENERATED LEGACY** series, follows the investigative skills of our reporter, *Stella*, into a world of intrigue, mystery and danger. With the support of *Jamie and DA*, she finds herself trying to convince her contact in the Government that unusual accidents are not quite what they seem. Can she uncover the details in time to save... The President of The United States?

NJLAL, the sixth and final book from Mickey Stone, a puzzle booklet, for those who have traveled along **The Venerated Legacy** path. Only the most worthy will solve the mysteries contained within; some ancient, some present... and all can be called by a simple word. ***TRUTH***.